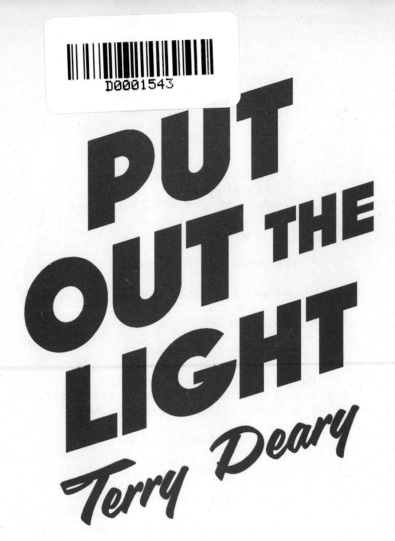

PUT OUT THE LIGHT

Terry Deary

A & C Black • London

First published 2010 by
A & C Black Publishers Ltd
36 Soho Square, London, W1D 3QY

www.acblack.com

Text copyright © 2010 Terry Deary

ISBN 978-1-4081-3054-4

A CIP catalogue for this book is available from the British Library.

This book is produced using paper that is made from wood
grown in managed, sustainable forests. It is natural, renewable and
recyclable.The logging and manufacturing processes conform
to the environmental regulations of the country of origin.

Printed and bound in Great Britain
by J F Print Ltd., Sparkford, Somerset.

Put out the light, and then put out the light.
From *Othello* by William Shakespeare

Since they are attacking our cities, we will wipe out theirs.
Adolf Hitler, German leader, speaking in August 1940 after the bombing of Berlin.

Never in the field of human conflict was so much owed by so many to so few.
Winston Churchill, British war leader, speaking in August 1940 about the Royal Air Force defence that became known as 'The Battle of Britain'. The pilots are remembered as 'The Few'.

August

1

**Sheffield, England
6 August 1940**

'Put out the light!' the warden cried.

'Put out the light!' we shouted after him.

It was dark in the alley and we hid in the shadows of the doors that led into the yards. He couldn't see us.

My sister Sally giggled. She was small and stupid and rather smelly. I suppose I wasn't daisy-fresh myself, but I always thought Sally smelled worse.

The streetlights were switched off. Heavy black curtains hung at every window. But from time to time, a chink of light escaped and the warden shouted, 'Put out the light!'

Every time he shouted, we shouted, too. A silly game, I know. But we were bored. It was the summer holidays. We had no school. No friends. Mine had all been sent away to the safety of the countryside. But not me. Not Sally. We stayed in Sheffield and waited for the bombs to fall. Bored.

The man turned at the end of the row of houses and began to walk down the alley. Most of the houses had their toilets there and it smelled worse than Sally on a bad day.

'Put out the light!' he cried, and before we could echo him, a yard door flew open and an old woman stuck her head out.

'Who's that? Who's that shouting? Clear off, you cheeky beggar. Clear off or I'll call the police.'

The man stopped. In the starlight, we could see him step towards her. He wore a long coat and a steel helmet like an upside-down soup plate. He pointed to the white letters on his helmet – ARP.

'Air Raid Precautions, Mrs Grimley,' he said. 'It's me, Warden Crane. I can see light in your window.'

'Of course you can see light. I'm reading the paper. I can't read in the dark. What do you think I am? A cat?'

'No, Mrs Grimley. But you have to draw the curtains tight. It's the blackout. You can be fined five pounds, Mrs Grimley. You wouldn't want that, would you?'

'Who says?' she snapped. Her white hair glowed like a halo and her round spectacles shone.

'The law, Mrs Grimley. Now, let me come and check that curtain and you'll stay out of trouble.'

'I've never been in trouble in my life,' she said as she led the way into the back yard.

Sally and I crept closer. The smell of the toilet made my eyes water.

'We don't want German bombers seeing your light and dropping a bomb on your head, do we?'

8

the warden said as they moved towards Mrs Grimley's kitchen door.

'Bombers? Bombers? There aren't no bombers,' she argued.

'No, but there could be at any time.'

'Why would they want to drop bombs on me? I never did nothing to them Germans.'

'True, but they'd send bombs to flatten the steelworks over at Tinsley,' the warden explained.

'Tinsley? We're two miles from Tinsley!'

'They might miss, and then where would you be?'

'In the shelter at the end of Stanhope Street,' she said sourly and closed the door behind them.

'That told him,' Sally said, laughing.

'You'd better watch he doesn't catch you,' I said to my little sister. 'He'll have *you* locked up.'

'Mum'll kill *you* if I get caught,' she said. 'She says you have to look after me.'

'I know,' I muttered. 'Oh, I know!'

And that was the night we *did* get caught.

Warden Crane left the house and walked to the end of the alley. 'Put out the light . . . and then put out the light!' he cried, and we called out, too. But he didn't seem to hear.

He turned onto the main road and we raced after him. But as we hurtled round the corner, we ran straight into his waiting arms. 'Now, you two, you've had your fun. Just run along home. It's ten o'clock.'

'Are you going to send us to prison?' Sally squealed.

'You think I should?' the warden asked. He was tall and broad and over sixty years old, I reckon. His hair was grey and just a little too long. It curled out under his helmet.

'You talk funny,' I said to him. 'I mean, the other wardens say, "Put that light out", but you shout, "Put out the light".'

'Shakespeare,' the warden said in a deep voice. 'He was a writer. He wrote great plays, but he's dead now.'

'In the war? Did a bomb fall on him?' my sister asked.

'No, he died over three hundred years ago. But actors like me still perform his plays. And one of his greatest plays was called *Othello*. A man creeps into his wife's room. . .' The warden's deep voice turned soft and low and spooky. 'He blows out the candle and then he smothers her. He says, "Put out the light, and then put out the light."'

'So he put out *two* lights?' I frowned.

'No, he put out the bedside candle and then he put out the light of her life – he murdered her.'

Sally shook herself free. 'You can't be an actor. You're a warden.'

'In the war, we do what we have to,' Warden Crane explained. 'In a lot of cities, even *children* work with the ARP service.'

'Shouting, "Put out the light"?' Sally asked.

'No, as messengers. I mean, if I see a fire, I can't run to the nearest telephone very quickly. I'm a bit old for that. But children make good runners. They can have the fire service out here before any real damage is done.'

'Can we be *your* runners?' Sally asked.

'Sheffield doesn't have runners,' he said. 'But when the bombing starts, you may be able to help me.'

'Do you think the bombing *will* start?' I asked.

'Bound to, lad – what's your name?'

'Billy. Billy Thomas, and this is my sister, Sally.'

'Yes, Billy. Sheffield steel makes planes and tanks. The enemy will want to put a stop to that. Oh yes, they'll be here any day, and we'll be ready for them.'

Of course, he was right.

2

Warden Crane walked off into the darkness. The new moon glinted on his shiny black helmet. We wandered past the end of the houses. There's usually a wind off the Pennines in Sheffield. It's a black-bricked, smoke-skied, wind-chilled steel town, where the factory chimneys rise across the skyline like broken teeth and the people can be hard as the metal made there. The wind made the ragged posters on gable ends flap. Some of the posters were selling stuff like Tetley's ale, Fry's chocolate (if your ration book let you buy the stuff), Woodbine cigarettes, John Bull tyres and Nugget boot polish.

I pointed to one at the top. 'Monkey soap. Hey, Sally, that would suit you!'

She pretended she hadn't heard.

There were new posters, too; posters about the war saying things like *Women of Britain, come into the factories* or *Dig for Victory* and a picture of a warden like Mr Crane telling off a little boy in a bombed street. He was saying, 'Leave this to us, sonny. You ought to be out of the city.' Mum and Dad had ignored that one.

Sally and I walked back down the alley and stopped near the door to Mrs Grimley's back yard.

'Come on, Sally,' I said. 'Mum says *Sexton Blake*'s on the radio tonight. He's the best detective in the world.'

'Not as good as Sherlock Holmes,' she argued. My sister liked to argue.

'Sherlock Holmes is dead,' I said. 'That makes Sexton Blake the best. We don't want to miss him.'

'Don't care,' she sniffed.

But before we could move, we heard the clatter of marching boots on the cobbles. The footsteps were getting closer.

A man walked down the alley towards us, just a shadow against the purple sky. He was whistling softly. As he drew nearer, his face became a pale oval. We could make out that he was a young man in uniform.

'Hello, kids. What are you doing out at this time?' The man peered down at us. He had a handsome face and I saw from the badges it was an Air Force uniform. The silver wings showed he was a pilot. My mouth went dry. A pilot. A *real* pilot.

'We're running,' Sally said.

The pilot blinked. 'Well, if you don't mind me saying, you're not running very fast. In fact, you look like you're standing still!'

'Very funny, ha ha!' Sally sneered. 'We are runners for Warden Crane. If there's a fire, we race to the fire station and get them here faster than a bullet from a cowboy's gun.'

'There aren't any fires here,' the airman said. 'So why are you hanging around?'

'What's it to you?' Sally asked rudely.

13

'Sally!' I croaked when I found my voice.

'This is my house and I have a right to ask who's standing at my back door,' he explained.

'Liar! Liar! Pants on fire!' Sally said, raising her voice. 'This is Mrs Grimley's house. We just saw her go inside.'

'And I am Paul Grimley. Ada's my mother. Now push off home before I call the zoo and have you locked up in a cage, like the little monkey you are.'

'Eeeeh! The cheek! Did you hear that, our Billy?'

'Let's go, Sally,' I murmured. She ignored me. Even under the thin moonlight I imagined I could be seen glowing red as a steel furnace. Little sisters usually show lads up, but Sally was the worst in the world.

'Why aren't you out shooting down German bombers?' my sister demanded.

'First, I can't see any bombers. And second, I'm a bomber pilot,' he explained.

'Ohhhh!' Sally sighed. 'They're boring. Fighter pilots are best. Our dad works at Firbeck air base and he says – stop pulling my sleeve, Billy – he says *fighter* pilots are the cream of the cream.'

'And my mum always says cream is full of clots,' the pilot said with a laugh. 'Now clear off!'

Before Sally could answer, I dragged her away. We heard the back door of the house open, and Mrs Grimley called, 'Is that you, our Paul?'

'Yes, Mum, I've got twenty-four hours' leave before we set off on the next mission.'

'Come on in then. Come and tell us all about it.'

The door closed and silence fell on the dark streets. Somewhere, a church clock chimed the hour.

'Sexton Blake!' Sally cried. 'He's on the radio now. He'll have solved ten murders if we don't hurry. We don't want to miss it.'

'I already *said* that,' I argued.

'He's better than Sherlock Holmes,' she told me.

'You said –' I began. But Sally was racing down the lane to the end of our street. Sometimes, I wished one of those murderers would get his hands on our Sally.

Sisters!

3

Dachau, Germany
6 August 1940

The teacher's eyes shone. 'Boys!' he cried and clapped his hands. 'Today our maths lesson is cancelled.'

'Hooray!' Manfred Weiss cried, jumping to his feet. No one else in the class had dared to move.

Herr Gruber, the teacher, turned red and glared at him. 'I will deal with you later, Weiss. I will cane you so hard that you won't sit down for a week.'

'Would I have to stand up to do my lessons, sir?' Manfred asked.

Manfred was a tall boy with a mop of brown hair and the round face of a baby. His small friend, Hansl, sat next to him and swallowed a choked cry. He wasn't sure if Manfred was being stupid or cheeky. But it was a dangerous way to talk to Herr Gruber.

The teacher breathed heavily. 'Stand up, boy. I look at you, Weiss, and I remember the story of the father who wrote to Herr Hitler. The father said his son was feeble-minded and asked Herr Hitler if he could kill him. And what did Herr Hitler say?'

'He said, "Yes",' Manfred replied.

'Exactly. This is still a maths lesson, Weiss, so let me give you a little test – it costs four marks each day to keep a feeble-minded person alive. There are

300,000 feeble-minded people in German asylums. How much would we save each day if we did not have to care for them?'

Manfred closed his eyes and thought. 'One million . . . and two hundred thousand marks.'

'Exactly, Weiss. The Nazi Party has plans to deal with the feeble-minded, Weiss. Be careful, or I will add you to the list of mental cases.'

Some of the boys giggled at Manfred's embarrassment, but Herr Gruber didn't seem to mind. He carried on as Manfred stayed on his feet. 'Every family has a black sheep. Luckily, *your* family also has a sheep as white as fresh snow.' Herr Gruber turned to the class. 'And we are honoured to have Weiss's brother, Ernst, here today.' He walked to the door and threw it open. 'Come in, Oberleutnant Weiss.'

A young man in the uniform of the German Air Force marched into the room. He looked uncomfortable under the gaze of forty boys and his high collar appeared too tight. The oberleutnant carried a rolled paper under his arm. He gave a sharp nod to the teacher, then turned to the class, pink-faced.

Herr Gruber said, 'We are one year into this war and we have many heroes – great German fighters like Oberleutnant Weiss. I invited him here today to tell us about life in the Luftwaffe and how we plan to invade Britain and end the war. Give him a round of applause, boys.'

The pupils clapped politely and the pilot tried to look modest. 'Good afternoon,' he said. 'I am Ernst Weiss and I am the captain of a bomber aircraft.'

'What sort?' a small boy at the back asked.

Weiss gave that sharp nod again and took the roll of paper from under his arm. He let Herr Gruber pin it to the blackboard. 'There are three main attack bombers in our squadron and here they are. It will be useful for you to know what they look like in case you see one flying over the city. If you see a large plane that does *not* look like one of these, it could be an enemy bomber, so you should run like hell!'

The boys laughed and the pilot pointed at the diagrams. 'We fly Junkers Ju 88s, Dornier Do 17s and Heinkel He 111s.'

Excited questions flew for an hour and the boys listened more eagerly than they ever did to Herr Gruber's maths lectures.

'Have you killed many English people?' Hansl asked.

Oberleutnant Weiss became serious. 'We do not want to kill English people,' he said quietly. 'First, we aim to wreck the airfields so they cannot send up planes to stop us from invading. Soon, we will send an army over in ships and barges to land on the south coast.'

'Operation Sealion,' little Hansl said. 'My father told me about it.'

The pilot nodded. 'We want to destroy the factories that make the tanks and aircraft, the shipyards that build the battleships, the power stations and the railway lines. We want the British army to suffer so much loss that they tell their government to surrender.'

'Like Germany had to in the last war,' Herr Gruber nodded.

'The women and children of England will not be hurt, unless a bomb has their name on it, of course,' Oberleutnant Weiss said.

'You put the names of women and children on your bombs, Ernst?' Hansl gasped.

'No, no, no,' the pilot cut in. 'It is an old belief. Everyone has a time to live and a time to die. If a bomb falls – or a bullet is fired – it will not kill you unless it is your time to die. We fly over England and the British send their Spitfires and Hurricanes to shoot us down. Some of my friends never return. It was their time to die.'

'Aren't you afraid?' the small boy at the back asked.

'What is the use? I cannot change a thing. It is fate. If it is not my time, then a thousand Spitfires cannot kill me. And if the British send aeroplanes to bomb our town, then *you* will be safe, unless a bomb has *your* name on it.'

The boys fell silent. The teacher rubbed his hands and said, 'Enough of this gloomy talk of death. You must have some other questions for Oberleutnant Weiss?'

'When will our army invade England?' Manfred asked.

'That is for our Führer, Herr Hitler, to decide,' the pilot said. 'It has to be before the end of September. The weather in the English Channel will be too stormy after that. But we must win the war in the air first.' Then with a small smile he added, 'When Herr Hitler has decided, you will be the first to know, Manfred. I will ask him to send a special messenger to our house to tell you.'

The boys laughed. They had a hundred other questions to ask, but Herr Gruber told them it was four o'clock and time to go home.

4

The pilot took his charts and left while the boys tidied the classroom and walked out in silence.

As they reached the yard, Manfred and Hansl heard screams – screams of excitement, screams of rage. They were not supposed to run in the school yard, but they sprinted over to the main gates.

They saw a crowd of girls from the school next door, gathered in a circle around something on the ground. Some girls were hurrying to the side of the road to pick up stones and mud. Then they rushed back to the circle to hurl the filth down.

Manfred pushed through the crowd and saw a small girl lying on the ground. Her eyes showed no fear and her face no pain, though her head was bleeding and her rough grey dress was torn.

The schoolgirls howled like wolves and some risked the stones to jump forward and aim a kick at their victim.

Manfred shouted in protest and forced his way to the front. As he dragged the small girl to her feet, a big blonde girl glared at him, her red face fierce. 'Traitor!' she screeched. 'Traitor! Helping an enemy of the state!'

Suddenly, the attacker's face vanished. Hansl had dragged her away and was now pulling at Manfred's arm. 'Let's go, Manfred,' he cried.

Manfred let Hansl lead him out of the circle, but still he gripped the small girl's wrist and dragged her after them. The schoolgirls began to follow the boys down the street, picking up stones and clods of grass on the way.

The red-faced girl raised an arm holding half a brick. Manfred waited to see if it would hit him or the small girl. But slowly she lowered her arm. The brick fell to the ground.

The other girls let their stones drop. They turned their backs on the boys and hurried away. The small girl in grey looked up at Manfred, sniffing back tears.

'It's all right,' Manfred said. 'You're safe.'

The girl shook her head and looked past the boys' shoulders. For the first time she looked afraid. Manfred swung round to see what had scared her. A policeman was walking towards them.

Manfred smiled at him. 'Good afternoon.'

The policeman ignored him and looked at the small girl. 'Why are you on the streets?' he asked. He was old and his face was parchment yellow.

The girl stood silently.

'You are making trouble.'

Manfred gasped. 'She wasn't doing anything, sergeant.'

'Constable. Constable Horst.'

'Constable Horst. Those girls were stoning her for no reason.'

The policeman glared at him. 'They had *every* reason. She is from the prison camp. See that red triangle sewn on her dress? You know what that means?'

'The prisoners who are enemies of the state wear red triangles,' Manfred shrugged. 'But a skinny girl can't do any harm!'

The policeman said, 'She probably came here with her family from Poland. Most red triangles are Polish prisoners. Is that right, girl?'

The girl gave a tiny nod, but her pale-grey eyes were as blank as ever.

'If her parents are in the camp, she should be working as a servant in the town. She has no right to be on the streets. Camp brats attract trouble like filth attracts rats. She could be spying.'

'Spying!' Hansl laughed.

The policeman's face turned red. 'Yes. Do not laugh, boy – a man was hanged in Munich last week for making a joke about the Nazi Party. I will report you to your block warden and he will visit your family to make sure they punish you.'

Hansl swallowed hard. The block warden looked after fifty families to make sure they were true to the Nazi way of life. A visit from him was a fearful event. 'Sorry, sir,' he muttered.

The policeman went on, 'There is a munitions factory in Dachau making bombs and shells and bullets for our troops. The prisoners work there. A girl like this can make a map. When the British bombers arrive, they will know exactly where to drop their bombs. Isn't that right, girl?'

The girl stared straight ahead.

'That is why you're on the streets. We are taking you into custody until we find whose house you work in and why you are out,' the man said.

'But she's just a kid!' Manfred gasped.

'You want to join her?' the policeman growled.

'No.'

'Then shut your mouth or you will.'

'I work in the factory,' the girl said suddenly. She spoke German with a strong accent.

The policeman sneered. 'You are too skinny to work with the machines. You're lying.'

'I sweep the floor. I make the tea.'

'And why are you outside the camp wall?'

The girl reached into the pocket of her dress and pulled out a piece of paper.

The policeman pulled out a pair of glasses and squinted through them. 'A coupon from the camp,' he nodded.

'What is that?' Hansl asked.

'We can't pay the prisoners money, can we? They might use it to help them escape. So we give them coupons they can exchange for goods in the shops. This one is for tea.'

'So, she was telling the truth?' Manfred said.

'Maybe,' the policeman said. 'Your papers, girl?'

She handed over a printed sheet and the policeman read it. 'Irena Kar—'

'Karski,' the girl muttered.

'Your papers are in order.'

'So you can let her go?' Hansl added.

The policeman looked weary. 'Commandant Zill would be angry if I arrested the camp's tea girl. So you can get on with your errand, Polish brat,' he said and gave her a push.

The girl ran down the street on legs as thin as a sparrow's.

The policeman looked hard at the boys. 'When the first bombs fall on Dachau, you will remember what Constable Horst told you.'

'My brother Ernst is in the Luftwaffe,' Manfred said. 'And he says the British won't bother with small towns like Dachau.'

'When the first bomb falls, you will remember,' the policeman repeated and walked away.

Cambrai Luftwaffe aerodrome, France
24 August 1940

Ernst Weiss sat in the largest room of the aerodrome waiting for his Luftwaffe commander to appear.

'What's the problem?' one of the pilots cried. 'The weather has cleared. We should be in the air, bombing airfields in England.'

'There'll be a good reason, don't worry,' Ernst told him. 'You mustn't be so impatient.'

'But we need to win the air war this week,' the pilot grumbled. 'Every day counts. Why aren't we out smashing the Royal Air Force now?'

'Good question,' said the commander, coming into the room. He wore an eye patch and walked with a limp, both injuries from the last war.

The pilots shuffled in their seats to face the front and fell silent.

'Good morning, gentlemen. Mark today in your diary as the day we smash little England. Air Marshall Göring has ordered Air Fleet 2 to bomb the main fighter airfields in the south of England. There will be nothing left of them by the time they have finished.'

The pilots groaned. 'But what about us? What about Air Fleet 3?' someone asked.

'The air marshall has given us the task of bombing the cities where fighter planes are built. But we will bomb them at night, when their Spitfires and Hurricanes can't stop us. Their blackouts will be useless – our X-Gerat wireless system will guide us anywhere we want.'

'And where are we going to bomb tonight?' Ernst asked.

The commander pointed to a map. 'Castle Bromwich here, near Birmingham, where they make the Spitfires. Another squadron will head for the Portsmouth docks and a third will raid the oil storage tanks at Thameshaven in London. Get some rest and we'll assemble here again at 1900 hours for final instructions. Dismissed.'

5

Over Munich, Germany
25 August 1940

It was hot inside the Wellington bomber. It smelled of burning oil and the booming of its two engines shook the crew.

The half-moon shone on the river below. A young man at a desk in the cabin shouted into the microphone in his mask. 'I know where we are! Head west five points, skipper.'

'West five points,' Paul Grimley echoed and twisted the control stick in his hand. 'So where are we, Sergeant Tench?'

'Near Munich, sir.'

'Munich! How did we ever get so far south?'

'It was when we dived to escape those fighters, sir. My maps and compasses were scattered. Sorry – I got us lost.'

Paul Grimley sighed. 'Never mind, young Alan. It's your first flight. You did well to get us to Berlin. Plot the shortest route home, and let's get some well earned kip, shall we?'

'We've enough fuel to get us home . . . just,' the engineer said. 'We need to be a bit lighter though.'

Another voice crackled in the earphones. 'We still have a bomb on board, sir.'

'Fine, Sergeant Kewell,' Officer Grimley said. 'Drop it now.'

'Yes, sir.'

The plane slowed as the bomb doors opened. There was a clatter as the bomb rolled out of the belly of the plane and the crew felt it leap upwards as the load fell away. The bomb doors closed and the plane headed back on the long flight home to England.

Somewhere, ten thousand feet below, the bomb fell and exploded with a flash. By then, the Wellington was two miles away and climbing into the safety of the high silver clouds.

RAF Mildenhall, Suffolk, England
26 August 1940

Landing the Wellington in near-darkness was a tricky job. Paul Grimley brought the plane down gently in a gusty side wind and taxied over to the hangar.

Wing Commander Parry was waiting for them. He was in full uniform and his thin moustache bristled like an angry walrus. He waited silently while the weary crew climbed down the steps to the ground.

Paul gave a tired salute. 'Morning, sir.'

'Where have you been?' Parry demanded. He had a Welsh accent that gave him a whining tone.

'Bombing Germany, sir.'

29

'Yes, but the rest of the flight were back seventy-three minutes ago.'

Paul rubbed his eyes. 'We usually meet in the morning to talk through the raids, sir. Can it wait till then? The lads are exhausted.'

Parry's eyes bulged and his lips curled back. 'Don't tell *me* when we should meet. I am your commander and *I* tell *you*. I want an explanation as to why you have been *joy-riding* around Germany in a valuable RAF plane when you should have been back *here*!'

'Being chased by a pack of Messerschmitt fighters isn't joy-riding,' the pilot said, a spot of red glowing in each cheek.

'Sir.'

Paul took a deep breath. The rest of his crew seemed to be holding theirs. 'Being chased by a pack of Messerschmitt fighters isn't joy-riding . . . *sir*.'

'Well?'

'I'm very well, sir. A little tired but a few hours sleep and I'll be right as rain,' Paul joked and his crew gave small smiles.

Wing Commander Parry stepped forward and jabbed the pilot in the chest. 'I meant, well . . . where is my explanation?'

Sergeant Tench saw Paul start to clench his fists. He stepped forward. 'It was my fault, sir. My charts got scattered on the floor when we rolled out of the fighters' way and it took me a while to get them sorted.'

Parry turned on him. 'Of all the stupid things to do. You risk a plane worth tens of thousands of pounds because you're a clumsy little oaf?'

'Sorry, sir.'

'You'll be sorry, all right. I'll have you on a charge. I'll have you locked away for a week till you've learned your lesson. You're nothing but a schoolboy. An ignorant, careless schoolboy.'

'Go easy on him, sir,' Paul put in. 'It was his first mission – until the war started, he *was* a schoolboy.'

Parry turned on the pilot. 'Don't tell me who I should or should not go easy on, Grimley, you northern, working-class slum boy.'

What happened next was so quick that Paul had trouble remembering how Wing Commander Parry ended up on the floor. Parry seemed to raise a hand to push Paul in the chest. Paul knocked Parry's hand aside with his left hand, then his right fist seemed to come up and punch the officer on the jaw.

The little Welshman staggered backwards and fell on the seat of his well-pressed trousers in a puddle of engine oil. 'In the last war they would have shot you for striking an officer,' Parry crowed. 'The very least you can expect is a long stretch in jail . . . slum boy.'

It took half an hour to drag Group Captain Flynn from his bed, get him dressed and into his office. He heard what everyone had to say and spoke quickly. 'Ten Wellingtons left here tonight and only nine returned. One crew was reported going down in flames. Young men died tonight. That is war. I flew Sopwith Camels in the last war. We got used to seeing planes go down. Sometimes they were flamers – if the pilot was lucky he was dead before the plane caught fire. If he was unlucky. . .' The group captain let the words hang in the still air.

The crew looked at their boots. They could all picture the horror.

'Anyway, we lost about a pilot a week. . . Never got used to it. But now, when one of these planes goes down, we lose a crew of six. *Six*. Gone in one crash. Six families destroyed and six young men dead doing their duty. Do you understand what matters most in this war? Getting home safely.'

'Yes, sir,' the men muttered.

'And what are you doing? Fighting like children. Six men die doing their duty and you're squabbling like dogs over a bone.'

'A pilot cannot strike an officer, sir,' Parry said.

'Get out.'

'But, sir –'

'Get out. Now! All of you except Grimley. Get some sleep. You'll be flying again tomorrow night.' He looked at the clock on his wall. 'Tonight, I mean.'

The men left.

'Sit down, Grimley,' Group Captain Flynn said. 'You look ready to fall over.'

32

'Thanks, Group Captain.'

Flynn took his chair from behind his desk and sat facing Paul Grimley so their knees almost touched. 'We need every pilot we can get. The Luftwaffe will attack any day now. It would be a stupid waste to have a good pilot like you locked away because you can't keep your temper.'

'Sorry, sir.'

'But I can't let you strike an officer and I can't have you working with Wing Commander Parry again.'

'No, sir.'

'I want you to write me a letter and ask for a transfer. You have a lot of anger, Sergeant Grimley, but I want you to take it out on the Nazis.'

Paul Grimley looked up into the tired old eyes of his commander. 'Yes, sir, but can I re-train, sir? Can I switch to a fighter squadron? I could really use my anger then. I don't like this job, dropping bombs where women and children might get hit.'

Flynn nodded slowly. 'Good idea, Grimley. You're from Sheffield, aren't you?'

'Yes, sir.'

'Fighter Command's number 13 group is up there. We'll have you flying Spitfires and Hurricanes in no time. And Grimley?'

'Yes, sir?'

'Don't go hitting your new commander. Next time he might hit you back.'

6

Sheffield, England
26 August 1940

'Put out the light!' Warden Crane cried a little wearily.

I stood next to Sally on the corner of the dark alley. The night sky was ink-blue, but the stars burned down on the cobbles and lit the washing-lines that were strung across the lane. A faint stream of light slipped through Mrs Grimley's curtains. We giggled. It was the same every night. Warden Crane walked to the back door and rapped on it till the ancient paint flaked off.

A minute later, the door flew open and light blazed over the cracked pavement, showing the warden's face twisted with pain. '"Frailty, thy name is woman",' he said to us. He turned to face the owner of the house. 'For goodness' sake, Mrs Grimley, how many times do I have to tell you?'

'Tell me what?'

'To keep your curtains closed!'

The old woman waved a bony finger under the warden's nose. 'My son Paul is in the RAF. He wrote a letter to say he's visiting me this week. And do you know what he says? He says bombers like to fly when the moon is full, so they can see where to bomb.' She raised her finger and pointed at the sky. 'See? Half-moon – no bombers.'

34

The warden sighed. 'The German planes don't need moonlight, Mrs Grimley,' he said.

'Don't they?'

'No.'

'Why not?'

'Because there are people in Sheffield who leave their curtains open and show them the way – people like you,' he growled. 'Now, if I catch you showing a light tomorrow, I *will* report you to the police. You'll go to court. You'll probably be fined five shillings.'

The old woman folded her arms across her skinny chest. 'Five shillings? I can afford that. You think I'm poor, do you? Just because I live in this shabby street? Well, let me tell you, young man, I don't have ten shillings in my best teapot . . . oh, no . . . I have ten *pounds*.'

The warden turned and looked across the street. The starlight caught his eyes as he stared straight at us. 'I wouldn't go shouting that around the street, Mrs Grimley. There are villains around who'll rob you soon as look at you.'

The woman sniffed. 'They can't rob me,' she crowed. 'They don't know where I hide me money.'

'In your teapot!' Sally called suddenly.

Mrs Grimley stepped onto the pavement and glared at my sister. 'How did you know that?' she screeched.

'I just heard you tell Warden Crane,' Sally said.

'Yes . . . well . . . my Bert died three years ago

and I collected his insurance. Hundreds of pounds. *Hundreds*. I'm not poor, you know. But it's so well hidden, no one will ever find it. No one.'

'Mrs Grimley, you really should keep your money in the bank, where it's safe,' the warden said, shaking his large head.

'Safe!' the woman spat. 'Banks get robbed! I've seen them.'

I pushed myself off the wall and wandered across the yard towards her. 'You've seen a bank getting robbed?'

'Oh yes, many times,' she told me.

'In Sheffield?' Sally asked.

'Yes, in Sheffield,' the woman said. 'At the Tinsley Picture Palace on Sheffield Road. Sometimes we went to The Pavilion on Attercliffe Common. I used to take our Paul – he's a bomber pilot, you know. We used to go and watch all those cowboy films. Our Paul used to love Tom Mix, but I liked the women.'

'Yes, Mrs Grimley, but those are just films—'

'*Adventures of Dorothy Dare*, *Ruth of the Rockies*, *A Lass of the Lumberlands* . . . but me favourite was *The Perils of Pauline*.'

The warden spread his hands and moaned. 'They are *films*. I'm an actor myself . . . and when I play Othello, I don't really smother my wife. It's not real life!'

Mrs Grimley looked slowly around. 'So,' she said

with a sly edge to her voice, 'are you saying nobody ever kills his wife?'

'No, but –'

'And are you saying no one robs banks?'

Warden Crane blew out his cheeks, 'No, I'm not saying no one robs banks –'

'There you are then!' the woman crowed. 'Banks get robbed. And they are not getting robbed when my money's in them.'

The warden shook his head wearily. 'Can you just take care to keep your curtains shut, *please*?'

What happened next was such a shock it still runs through my head like one of those old black-and-white films. First, there was a low whirring sound, like a distant foghorn. It grew louder and the note got higher until it was a wail.

The warden jumped into the middle of the street. 'Air raid!' he shouted as doors crashed open and people tumbled outside. Then there was a foot-scuttering, foot-fleeing, breath-gasping, clog-clattering, door-slamming race to the shelters. The dark, empty street was suddenly filled with people and light, as they forgot to switch off their lights before they opened their doors.

As families streamed towards us, Warden Crane bellowed over the air-raid siren. 'Gas masks. If you haven't got your gas masks, go back and get them NOW!'

The stream of people turned into a blundering mass of struggling families. Some tried to turn back for their gas masks. Some crowded round the warden and babbled their questions.

'Stanhope Street,' he shouted. 'Go to the public shelter in Stanhope Street.'

'Where's that?' a woman asked. She was carrying a sleepy toddler in her arms and another tugged at the hem of her dressing gown.

'I'll show you,' Sally offered.

Warden Crane nodded at her. 'Good lass. You and your brother show them the way.'

He stood in the middle of the cobbles like a rock in a stream as people flowed around him.

'What about you?' I asked, hanging back.

'I need to check every house in the district. Make sure no one's asleep or too deaf to hear the siren.'

'You could get hit by a bomb,' I gasped.

The warden raised his chin in the air and looked as brave as Roy Rogers himself. 'It's my duty, lad. When the blast of war blows in our ears, then imitate the action of the tiger. Some of us have to risk our lives so the rest of you stay safe. Now, run along to the shelter.'

I turned and raced down the street. Sally stood at the corner, her voice as thin as one of the recorders we played in school. 'This way, down to the end of Stanhope Street!'

When the last family had passed, we walked behind them and went into the brick shelter with the concrete roof. It was like walking into an oven. The shelter was meant for fifty people but about two hundred were crowded inside. The smell was awful and the squalling children must have done more damage to the concrete roof than a ten-ton bomb. Men and women were arguing loudly about who should be allowed to sit on the stone floor. Some looked like they were going to faint in the crush and smoke, as fifty people lit up cigarettes.

Sally and I backed out into the road and were glad of the cool night air. The siren had faded. There was no sound of bombers. Then the wail began again, but this time a steady sound that meant all clear.

I stuck my head into the shelter. 'False alarm!' I cried through the wall of noise. As the word spread, there was more shouting as people were crushed in the rush to get out again. At last, people began to drift away.

'I'm staying in the house next time,' a man grumbled. 'I've got one of them Morrison shelters.'

'They're just a steel table,' a woman argued. 'Useless. I'm going to get an Anderson shelter put up in the back garden. I just wish I had a man to help.'

'I wish I had a garden,' the man said. 'Tell you what, *I'll* put up your shelter if you let me use it when there's a raid.'

'Would you do that?' the woman asked.

'Anything's better than going in there again,' said the man, as they walked off into the night.

Sally and I followed Mrs Grimley back up her road. 'There was never any raid,' she crowed. 'I *told* Warden Crane. I said, they need a bomber's moon.'

The old man who hobbled along beside her said, 'Ah, that was last night.'

'Last night?'

'I heard it on the radio,' the old man said. 'Last night we sent Wellington bombers over to Berlin.'

'Where's that?'

'Capital of Germany. Where that Mr Hitler lives.'

'Nasty man. Never liked his face. Silly moustache,' Mrs Grimley said.

'It'll be a burned moustache if our lads in the Wellingtons hit the target.'

'Oh, they'll hit the target all right,' the old woman said smugly. 'My Paul's a pilot in them bombers. I hope he got back safe.'

'Trouble is,' Mr Crawley said, 'it's a bit like poking a stick in a beehive.'

'Why would you want to do that?' Sally asked him.

'Stirring up trouble, if you ask me,' Mr Crawley said. 'If we attack them, then they'll attack us. Mark my words, the next time that siren sounds, it won't be a false alarm.'

7

Dachau, Germany
26 August 1940

Hansl stood in the street and looked at the rubble where once there had been a row of houses. 'Remember what you said yesterday?' he said.

Manfred nodded. 'My brother Ernst said the British won't bother with little towns like Dachau.'

'He was wrong,' Hansl said.

Manfred shook his head slowly. 'It was just one plane. Just one bomb. Ernst says it was a freak – probably some British plane losing some weight. There was a raid on Berlin last night.'

'We're a long way from Berlin,' Hansl mocked.

'Maybe he was lost.'

'How many are dead in Dachau?'

'Ten so far. Three missing. Five in hospital.'

'And your grandpa?'

'He refused to go to the shelter when the siren went off. He said he'd faced the British in the trenches twenty years ago and they didn't get him then, so they won't get him now.'

'He was wrong,' Hansl said.

'He's not dead. He's in hospital. Herr Gruber says I can have the morning off school to visit him.'

'Awwww!' Hansl cried. 'Some people have all the

luck. I wish my grandpa had been bombed and I got a morning off school. Even better, I wish that British plane had dropped a plane on the school and flattened Herr Gruber.'

'I'll send a letter to Mr Churchill with a map telling him to send two bombs – one for the school and one for your grandpa's house.'

'Will you?' Hansl gasped.

'No.'

Men and women were tugging at the rubble and loading it onto horse-drawn wagons. 'In a week, this street will be flat,' a policeman said. 'In a month, brand-new houses will have been built. The British will not break our spirit with their bombs. But we will break theirs. We will bomb them to dust. They deserve it.'

The town-hall clock struck nine. 'I'll be late!' Hansl cried, and raced down the street.

'You'll be late, too,' the policeman said to Manfred.

'I've got the morning off. They pulled my grandpa out of the rubble, so I'm off to visit him in hospital.'

'A good man, Weiss.'

'You know him?'

'Of course. We fought together in the trenches. He was as tough as a boot. Fifty bombs couldn't hurt him.'

'That's what he says,' Manfred nodded. 'How does he know?'

The policeman chuckled. 'You ask him. And tell him Inspektor Finkel was asking after him.'

'I will,' Manfred promised and walked away from the ruined street. The wind blew clouds of cement dust after him and the smell of burned wood filled his nostrils.

The hospital was a collection of low, wooden buildings housing different wards. A nurse pointed Manfred towards the emergency building. His grandpa had a bandage around his head that covered one eye and his arm was in a sling. His one blue eye shone fiercely. 'See, Manfred!' he cried as the boy stepped into the room. 'They can't get me. They couldn't get me in the last war and they won't get me now.'

'But they *did*, Grandpa,' Manfred said.

The old man scowled. 'They didn't *kill* me,' he argued. 'A bullet or bomb hasn't been made that has my name on it. When I was a boy, a gypsy looked at the palm of my hand and said I had the longest lifeline she'd ever seen. I'll live to a hundred – no bullets or bombs can change that.'

Manfred shivered. 'Herr Hitler says gypsies are under-humans. They're like the Polish and the Jews. They should be locked away in a camp so we don't have to mix with them.'

'Maybe,' the old man sighed. 'But I believed the gypsy that told me my fortune. It gives you great courage. I went into battle and I knew I'd be safe.

That's why I won an Iron Cross for bravery.' Suddenly, he stretched out a strong hand and gripped Manfred's wrist. 'When they dig up the ruins of the house, see if they can find my medal, there's a good lad.'

'Yes, Grandpa,' Manfred promised.

But, as he walked back to school, he forgot his promise. Manfred was too full of a new scheme and he couldn't wait to share it with Hansl.

Hansl was in the school canteen, dipping a piece of hard bread in a bowl of thin soup. Manfred grabbed a plate and sat beside his friend.

'What's wrong?' Hansl asked.

'Wrong?' Manfred said.

'You look agitated.'

'I have a plan to help us win this war. We will kill an Englishman!'

Hansl let a piece of soggy bread drop into his soup, splashing the wooden table. 'What? Grab a gun? *Steal* a gun, walk to France, find a boat and sail over to England? Shoot the first Englishman we see? Did the bomb hit you on the head? Are you mad?'

'No, listen, people are saying you only get killed if your name is on a bomb or a bullet.'

Hansl's face screwed up with a frown. 'So?'

'So, we find a bomb and we write an Englishman's name on it. Easy!'

'Which Englishman?' Hansl asked.

Manfred spread his hands. 'My grandpa says he

used to fight the Tommies in the last war. We find a bomb, we write Tommy on it and it's sure to kill a Tommy. Simple.'

Hansl nodded. 'Yes, Manfred. Simple. You are very, very simple. Maybe the doctor can have a look at your head.'

'What's wrong with my plan?'

Hansl ticked off the problems on his fingers. 'How do you write on a bomb?'

'With chalk. We steal a piece from Herr Gruber's classroom.'

'Where do we find a bomb?'

'There's a munitions factory just outside the work camp. It has hundreds of bombs,' Manfred said.

'How do we get into the factory? The guards will stop us at the gate.'

'They aren't proper guards. I mean, the real soldiers are at the front, fighting for Herr Hitler. The guards they leave behind are old men like my grandpa.'

'But they still have guns and they'll still keep us out,' Hansl argued.

'I've thought of that. We'll get a letter that says we can enter the factory – that it's part of our Hitler Youth training.'

Hansl shook his head. 'Shall I tear a piece of paper from my exercise book? Write you a note? They won't fall for it, Manfred.'

'No – my *brother* will write the note. He'll type it

on a piece of proper paper from his base, then he'll sign it. The guard won't dare stop us.'

Hansl blinked. 'It might work, but wait . . . How do we know where to find the bombs that are heading for England? There are thousands of bombs in the factory and it's huge.'

Manfred gave a small, tight smile. 'I've thought of that, too.'

As they walked to class, Manfred explained more. Hansl nodded. 'Yes, Manfred, it might just work. Let's wait and see.'

8

The school monitor rang the bell and the boys shuffled to their desks, waiting to be given the word to go.

Herr Gruber walked across to the old piano in the corner. 'The anthem, before you go, boys,' he said.

The class stood and raised their arms in the Nazi salute as their thin voices sang the marching song:

'Germany, Germany above all,
Above all in the world!'

The teacher stood at the door and watched the boys walk silently past him. As Hansl reached the door he said, 'Sir, is that an English spy in the corridor?'

'What?' the teacher gasped and turned to look. As he stepped out of the room, Hansl ran to the blackboard, snatched a piece of chalk and hid it in his pocket before hurrying after Manfred.

The two friends ran across the school yard laughing, their boots clacking in time as they sang:

'Manfred and Hansl above all,
Above all in the world!'

When they reached the street corner, Manfred skidded to a stop and leaned against the grocer's shop.

Some girls from the school next door wandered past, chattering, whispering and giggling as they caught sight of the boys waiting there.

The big blonde girl with the red face walked past and sneered, 'Traitor.'

'Are you really blonde, or do you dye your hair?' Manfred asked.

The girl turned redder and pretended she hadn't heard him.

When the group of girls had left, the small girl in the grey dress stepped into the street, nervous as a rabbit. She shuffled towards the grocery store.

Manfred moved into her path. 'Stop,' he said, unsure how to address her.

The girl stood stiffly, her head lowered and body hunched, as if ready for a beating.

'Irena Karski?'

'Yes, sir.'

'I'm not a sir,' Manfred said. 'I'm just Manfred, and this is Hansl. Remember? Two weeks ago? We helped you when those girls attacked you.'

'Thank you, sir.'

'Manfred.'

'Thank you, Manfred, sir.'

'I thought you might be able to help us in return.'

'I have to get back to the factory,' she said and tapped the red badge. 'If I'm gone too long they will beat me.'

Manfred nodded. 'Can you leave the factory any other time?'

She shrugged her bony shoulders. 'At night. There is a change of guard. The kind guard comes on duty. He used to let me go to the camp to see my father.'

'Tonight?' Manfred asked. 'Can you get out tonight?'

The girl raised her head and looked at him for the first time. 'Yes. But *you* can't. There's a curfew. You can't be on the streets after dark.'

Manfred gave a smile, looking braver than he felt. 'That doesn't bother me. Just tell me which gate and what time.'

'Gate C at 10 o'clock, sir.'

'We'll be there,' Manfred said and the girl slipped past him into the grocery store.

Hansl looked at his friend. 'No, *we* won't be there,' he said. 'I'm not getting shot for this. Writing on a bomb's a great idea, but it's not worth getting shot for.'

'Are you a coward?' Manfred jeered.

'Yes,' Hansl nodded.

9

Manfred pushed open his window and climbed out into the warm night. The town lay in darkness but a half-moon showed a faint cloud of dust over the bombed street where workers still dug in the rubble. He climbed down the drainpipe and dropped onto the soft grass before stepping out of the back gate and into the quiet lane. He had a torch with a blue bulb, but he didn't need it yet – the streetlights' tiny green flames were enough.

Manfred hadn't walked far when he heard feet on the road. A group of four soldiers marched in step down the middle of the street and he backed down an alley, hoping they wouldn't see him. He waited until they had turned a corner before stepping out.

'Where are you off to, young man?' a voice asked.

Manfred had almost walked into the old policeman. He choked back a scream and forced a smile onto his face. 'My grandpa –'

'What about him?'

'He asked me to check his bombed house – to see if I could find his medal from the last war.'

'At night?'

'It's the only time I have,' Manfred said in a voice that he hoped would soften the policeman's heart.

The parchment face peered at him closely. 'Your grandfather is a good man – ask Oberleutnant Siegel if the searchers have found anything. Tell them Constable Horst sent you.'

Manfred managed a smile. 'Thank you, Constable Horst. Thank you.' He was almost bowing as he backed away. He turned and ran down the street.

Manfred dodged around a bus that showed its ghostly blue headlights and reached his grandpa's house. The men lifting the broken bricks and timbers onto the carts were thin, with hollow eyes and ragged uniforms. They were slaves from the camp up the road. They worked in silence by the light of the moon. Some shone blue torchlight into the ruins.

The ruined houses were almost cleared now. Manfred saw his grandpa's living room standing open to the evening air. The furniture was covered in dust and mostly broken, but he knew it well. A ring of soldiers with machine guns stood around and watched. He guessed that the soldier with a pistol by his side was the officer in charge. He explained his search and Oberleutnant Siegel let him step over the shattered wall into the living room. He found the dining table and tugged at the drawer. The medal was there. Grandpa used to take it out every Sunday when Manfred called to see him.

Manfred waved it at the officer and called his thanks before he turned and ran up the road to the factory outside the camp. He used to play football in the surrounding fields before the war so he knew the layout. The church clock was chiming ten as he raced over the grass towards a gate in the high wire fence that had a sign saying 'C' over it.

The girl was already there, talking to a guard who sat on the ground rolling a cigarette. She said something to the man. He nodded and she stepped out to meet Manfred.

'What do you want with me, Manfred, sir?' Irena asked.

They began to walk away from the gate and into the moonlit field.

'I want you to get me inside the factory.'

The ghost of a smile twitched at the girl's thin lips. 'Most of the workers want to get *out* of the factory,' she said.

Manfred explained his plan to write a name on a bomb with chalk. The girl looked him in the eye. 'And me? Why should I do this for you?'

'I saved you from those girls. They could have killed you.'

'Maybe it would have been better if they did,' she said quietly.

'No!' Manfred cried. 'Life is hard now. But the war will soon be over. We are winning.'

'We?'

'Germany.'

'I am a Pole – an under-human, you call us,' Irena reminded him.

'But you can be proud to work for the greatest nation the Earth has ever seen,' Manfred said.

'Work, sir? You mean *slave*?'

'We Germans will treat you well after the war.'

'Thank you, sir.'

'You'll see. Look at the sign on the main gate. It says: "Work and you shall be set free". Help us to make bombs to win the war. When the war is over –'

'What then?'

'You can go back to Poland with your family and work just as you did before the war,' Manfred said.

The girl looked at him curiously, the moon lighting her large eyes and making deep shadows in her hollow cheeks. 'No, Manfred, sir, it *won't* be the same. I have no family. My family fought back when you Germans invaded.' Her voice was flat. 'You shot my mother because she spat on a German soldier. My father took a bullet in the chest when his gang of partisans attacked a German convoy in the woods. I nursed him till he was fit to walk, but a German patrol found us and shipped us here to work in the munitions factory.'

'But there are doctors at Dachau camp. We Germans wouldn't harm a good worker.'

Irena gave a small frown. 'You are right. It was not the Germans who killed him. It was the kapos.'

'What are they?'

'The Germans are too busy fighting the war to run the camp. They leave it to the prisoners to run themselves. The Germans picked the most cruel criminals to be kapos – to order us around, feed us, pick work parties and punish us when we don't work hard enough. The German guards are bad – but the kapos are much worse.'

'They killed your father?'

'He was weak – he only had one lung. They sent him to the gravel pits to shovel gravel twelve hours a day. I saw him every night after work.'

She stopped, closed her eyes and raised her face to the half-moon. Manfred saw one silver tear slide out through the closed lids. She sniffed and went on. 'One evening, he wasn't there. One of the Poles told me what had happened. When father fell over, too weak to work, a kapo marched him into the pond in the middle of the pit and made him stand in the water up to his chest. It was last December. When he fell forward, he was dragged out and put in a wheelbarrow. He was dead before they got him back to the camp.'

Manfred's voice was hoarse. 'The kapos . . . yes. Germans wouldn't treat a man like that, even an under-human.'

'Of course not,' Irena said quietly. 'Of course not.'

'So now you work in the factory?'

She nodded. 'But one day I will –'

'What?'

'I can't tell you. You will tell the guards and I'll be executed.'

'I'd never do that!'

She shrugged. 'What does it matter? I dream that one day I will escape. I will go to England. I'll be free.'

Manfred said eagerly, 'Then if you help me get into the factory, I will help you escape.'

'You can't.'

'I'll do my best. I promise.'

Irena looked at him. 'Perhaps,' she said. 'Perhaps.'

Cambrai Luftwaffe aerodrome, France
27 August 1940

The Luftwaffe pilots gathered in the main hall at the airfield. The commander spoke softly. 'Our air raids are smashing Britain thanks to the X-Gerat radio-beam system that's guiding our bombers to the targets. The British don't know a thing about the radio beam. If they did, they'd find a way to block it or bend it. If your plane is forced to crash-land in England, make sure you destroy the beam-tracking machine.'

'Yes, sir,' the pilots said as one.

'But we also need to check that the X-Gerat beam is really working. We need to send in a spy. We'll drop him soon after an air raid and get him to report back on how much damage we've really done. Luftwaffe command have asked for one of you to take the spy in. It will be a secret flight, so you'll have no cover from the Messerschmitt fighters. You'll be flying low to avoid their radar. It will be dangerous. Does anyone want the job?'

'I do,' Ernst Weiss said cheerfully. 'It sounds like fun!'

'You will leave some time in the next week, Weiss.'

Ernst gave a grim smile. 'I want a real adventure before we win this war.'

The commander nodded. 'If all our airmen were as brave as you, Weiss, we'd win it tomorrow.'

September

10

**Sheffield, England
1 September 1940**

Sundays were always bad. The shops were closed, and I had to go to Sunday school with our Sally. Real school was starting again on Monday, so at least that meant football in the yard to look forward to, and games of marbles and swapping cigarette cards with the other lads – the ones who hadn't been evacuated. But Sunday school was no fun at all.

The streets were empty as we trudged along to the church hall. 'Is Jesus up in the sky?' Sally asked.

I peered into the clouds and saw twenty or so of the huge, grey balloons on steel cables swaying in the wind. 'Yes,' I told her. 'He's sitting on top of that barrage balloon watching you. Make sure you behave.'

My sister punched me on the arm. 'Stop being silly, Billy. I want to know. Is Jesus up in the sky?'

'That's what the vicar said last week,' I reminded her.

'So why doesn't he just stop Mr Hitler's bombers? Why doesn't he reach down, pick them up and drop them in the sea?' she asked.

'Ask him,' I muttered.

Sally walked on, her heels clacking on the pavement. 'He's scary,' she said. 'Have you seen the hairs in his nose? I don't know how he breathes through them all.'

'And his ears!' I nodded. 'He says Jesus called him to be a vicar. I'm surprised he heard through that forest of hair!'

I laughed and ran to the church gate. The tumbledown tombstones were green and yellow with moss. A few flowers brightened the place and the wild spikes of willowherb glowed pink between the grey stones.

Sally stopped and gasped. 'Here, Billy! What would happen if a bomb fell in the graveyard?'

I shrugged. 'All the bodies would be blown to bits and scattered around.'

'And *splattered* around! There'd be legs on the roof and eyeballs stuck to the windows,' Sally cried, getting excited. 'It would be raining fingers and toes. Gruesome!'

The vicar, Mr Treadwell, was waiting at the door to the church hall like one of the gargoyles carved on the church roof. He wore a black coat that reached to his ankles, buttoned down the front, and had a black hood like a monk's – a cowl – over his shoulders. He was a hairy-nosed, dragon-breathed, greasy-haired, food-stained-shirt, scuffed-shoe, grey-faced man.

'What's gruesome?' the vicar asked.

'A bomb dropping in your graveyard,' Sally said.

'The dead won't mind. They are at rest with God,' he said with a sad smile and looked up. He smelled of the mouldering prayer books that sat in a pile by the church door. I wondered if he could smell himself.

'Our Billy says Jesus is sitting on one of them barrage balloons, watching us,' Sally said. 'Is that right, vicar?'

The man frowned and his heavenly look turned to thunder. 'Get inside,' he snapped. 'Sit down and be quiet.'

We followed him into the church hall. Sally whispered, 'I'm going to ask him why Jesus makes people with loads of hair inside their noses.'

'Don't you dare!' I squeaked in panic. 'You show me up again and I'll kill you.'

Sally sniffed. 'Our dad's a policeman. If you kill me, he'll catch you and they'll hang you like that Doctor Crippen who murdered his wife.'

'Dad won't do that,' I hissed. 'He knows what you're like. He'll probably make sure they give me a medal.'

'Well then, I'll go to heaven and I'll get Jesus to make sure one of them German bombs drops on your head.' Sally poked out her tongue as we sat in the second row of creaking wooden chairs that were as hard as Sheffield steel.

'You won't be seeing Jesus, because if I kill you, you'll go straight to hell.'

There were only a few children in the dusty hall, but they made enough noise. Once the hall had been full and the smell had been worse than fifty vicars, especially in winter when they didn't have baths. Lots of the kids had newspapers sewn into their vests to keep out the cold. When spring came their mothers cut them off, gave the kids a bath and washed off four months' worth of lice. But not Sally and me. Our dad was a policeman and he said we had to have a bath every week, the same as him.

'Enough!' roared the vicar, putting up his hand for quiet. 'I have some important news.'

The handful of children sat up and listened with open mouths as Vicar Treadwell spoke in a low voice. 'Yesterday German bombers flew over London. They were aiming to destroy the dockyards on the river. . . Does anyone know what the river in London is called?'

'Please, sir, the River Thames,' Jimmy Duncan said. He liked showing off, did Jimmy Duncan.

'Correct. But many bombs missed the docks and fell on houses in the East End of the city. Some were HE bombs . . . and that means?'

'High Explosive,' Jimmy said.

'Correct – they mostly explode before they hit the ground so the roofs of houses and factories are damaged,' the vicar nodded. 'The bombers then drop incendiaries.'

I put up my hand and said, 'They're bombs that

burst into flames and burn everything they touch.'

'Correct, and because the HE bombs have blown away the roofs, the incendiaries fall *inside* the houses and send them up in flames. Your Morrison shelters may save you from falling tiles and bricks, but they won't save you when an incendiary burns your rooms. You will be turned to cinder before you can get to the door. Your gas masks will melt and burn. They ambulance crews won't find enough of you to bury!'

One of the girls gave a whimper of fear. 'That's awful!' she moaned.

Even my tough little sister had turned pale. I could see her skin go white under her freckles.

'Two thousand Londoners were killed or injured yesterday. Some of the injured had bits of their bodies blown away and some were so badly burned they will die.'

'Urrrrgh!' I moaned. 'What's this got to do with God and Sunday school?' I asked.

Vicar Treadwell turned his long nose towards me and snorted through the grey forest of hair. 'You should not be here,' he said. 'Last year, you were all offered the chance to go to the countryside where it is safe – Lincolnshire. A beautiful, quiet part of England. But some of your parents refused to send you there. London was struck by the curse of the Devil last night. Sheffield will be next. Leave now, leave tomorrow – before I have to bury you in my churchyard.'

61

'Please, sir,' Eddie Duncan interrupted. 'I went to a farm. It was awful. They made us work picking tatties from first light till it got dark. And all we got to eat was bread and cheese. And we had to sleep in a barn with rats, so my mum brought us home!'

The vicar narrowed his eyes and spoke softly. 'Would you rather sleep with a rat or with an incendiary bomb turning your skin as crisp as pork crackling, Eddie?'

'Well. . . ' Eddie blinked.

'And you, Billy Thomas?' he asked me. 'A rat or a bomb? And you, Sally Thomas? Would you like to burn?'

My sister shrugged. 'Billy said I was going to burn in hell so I may as well get used to it.'

Vicar Treadwell turned purple with rage. 'Do not mock the word of the Lord!' he screamed and his breath smelled worse than the dead rats I'd seen in our back yard. 'The Lord says, "I will stretch out my hand, that I may smite thee and thy people with pestilence; and thou shalt be cut off from the Earth . . .'"

Sally jumped to her feet. 'If you smite me, my dad'll smite you back.'

'". . .When I sharpen my flashing sword and my hand grasps it in judgment, I will take vengeance on my adversaries and repay those who hate me . . .'" the vicar raged.

'Please yourself,' Sally said, 'but you're not getting

me to Lincoln with cheese and rats and dirty farmers.'

'". . . Let death seize upon you, and may you go down quick into hell . . ."' he spat.

Sally walked over to the door. 'I'll probably see you there,' she said.

I stumbled after her, muttered, 'Sorry,' to the vicar and ran down the path after my sister.

11

'You've done it now, Sal!' I cried.

'Done what? Nobody says we have to go to Sunday school.'

'Our ma says we have to,' I reminded her.

She sniffed. 'I'm not scared of Ma.'

'Yes, you are. When you get home early, she'll want to know why.'

'Well . . . well, I won't go home,' she said and turned to walk down the back alley behind Jubilee Terrace.

Mrs Grimley was in her yard. She had a mat hanging over the washing-line and was beating it till dust clouds drifted down.

'Hello, Mrs Grimley,' Sally called happily.

'Hello, pet,' the old woman said. 'Not in Sunday school?'

'Walked out,' Sally said proudly. 'That vicar was trying to boss us around. Telling us we had to get evacuated.'

'He always was a bossy one,' the woman nodded. 'Our Paul walked out just the same when he was a lad.' She shook her head and looked at the carpet beater. 'Makes a habit of it.'

'Sorry?' I said.

'He's just walked out of the bomber squadron.'

'He's left the RAF?' I gasped.

'No, no, no!' she cried. 'Mrs Meldrum came round

this morning. She has a telephone in her house. She said our Paul wanted to speak to me. He had some good news – said he was moving to Firbeck air base. Why, that's not twenty miles away. I'll get to see him more often.'

'But Firbeck is for *fighter* planes. Your Paul flies bombers. There aren't any bombers at Firbeck,' I told her. 'Our dad gave up his job with the Sheffield police to join the military police at Firbeck. He guards the fighters.'

'I know – it's all on account of that raid on London last night. Mr Churchill's been on the radio. He said it was wrong of them Germans to bomb British people in their homes. He said our Royal Air Force has to go across to Germany tonight and bomb *their* people. Well, our Paul said that's not right. He said he'd resign rather than kill women and children. Now the RAF doesn't want to lose a good pilot, so they asked if he'd train as a fighter pilot, shooting down Mr Hitler's bombers. So he's coming up on the train tomorrow. I'll be glad to see him. There's things I want to have a word with him about.'

'What things?' Sally asked.

'Wicked things,' the old woman sighed. 'You remember on Monday how the siren sounded and we all went down to the shelter on Stanhope Street?'

'Yes,' Sally and I nodded.

'When I got back, I thought my old teapot had

moved – the one I keep me money in. Nobody knows I keep ten pounds in that.'

'*We* knew that,' Sally said.

'We heard you tell Warden Crane,' I reminded her.

'Did you now? Well, in that case you might know what happened to me money. When I counted it, there were just nine pounds in the pot.' Her eyes narrowed. 'Maybe you know where my pound note went!'

'Are you saying we're thieves?' Sally shouted. 'Our dad's a policeman. We've never stolen a biscuit off a dog.'

Mrs Grimley spread her hands. 'You knew where the money was – it must have been you. I forgot I told you where it was.'

'We were in the shelter with you!' Sally raged. Her face was turning red. Curtains on the houses were moving as people looked out to see what the noise was.

'Let's go home, Sally,' I said and tugged at the sleeve of her cotton dress.

'I'm going nowhere till that witch says she's sorry,' Sally cried.

'Home, Sally . . . now!' I said and pulled harder.

'That's right – flee the scene of the crime,' the woman said and swished at us with her carpet beater. 'Come here and I'll give you the hiding of your lives, you little villains. I'm not the only one who's lost money when the sirens have gone off . . . I bet you did *all* the robberies.'

Sally's heels were sparking off the cobbles as she struggled to get free and rush at the woman. It was like trying to hold on to an eel. 'It wasn't us,' I said firmly. 'And I can prove it.'

'How?' Mrs Grimley asked, a little surprised.

My mouth opened and closed like a goldfish out of water. 'Er . . . er . . . I can prove it by . . . finding the real thief!' I finally managed to say.

Sally stopped struggling. 'Can you?' she asked.

'Dad's a policeman,' I said. 'If he can track down thieves, then anyone can,' I laughed, though I wasn't as confident as I sounded. 'I'll get your money back, Mrs Grimley, don't you worry.'

'It's not me pound note I worry about,' she said. 'It's me fortune that's hidden where you scallywags can't find it.'

I sighed. 'I'll catch the thief and stop him before he does,' I promised.

Mrs Grimley looked sour. 'I'll believe it when I see it. But my Paul will be back soon. He'll take you up in one of his aeroplanes and throw you out. That'll teach you to go robbing an honest woman.' She shut the back gate firmly.

'Where do we start looking for a burglar?' Sally asked.

'What do you mean "we"?' I asked her.

'Every detective needs someone to help them.'

Sally's eyes glowed. 'I'll be Sherlock Holmes and you can be Dr Watson.'

'Hang on,' I argued. '*I* should be Sherlock Holmes.'

'You *should*,' she agreed, 'but I bagged Sherlock first.' She ran down the alley. 'Come on, Dr Watson. We'll call Dad and get him to help.'

'I'm Sexton Blake and you're Paula Dane – his helper,' I shouted after her. But Sally was racing for home.

As I reached the kitchen door, I heard Sally call, 'What's for dinner, Ma?'

'Lamb,' Mum told her.

'Lamb! That must have taken every coupon in our ration books,' Sally sighed. 'Did you hear that, Billy? We're having a leg of lamb for Sunday dinner.'

I picked up two slimy balls that sat on the kitchen table and clutched one in each hand. 'I don't think so, our Sally,' I said. 'See what I have here?' I opened my hands.

'Urrrrgh! They're disgusting. They look like eyes!'

'Well done, Mr Holmes – that's just what they are. *Sheep's* eyes. And they're your dinner.'

Sally pulled a face and turned to Mum. 'Aw, Ma! Tell him to stop! Tell him! He says he's got sheep's eyes.'

Mum shrugged. 'He has. I got a sheep's head at the butcher and I'm boiling it up for dinner. I took the eyes out first because I didn't think you'd want them staring up at you from the plate.'

I closed and opened my right hand a couple of times. 'Look, Sherlock – this one's winking at you.'

Sally stamped out of the kitchen, disgusted.

'I'd have liked a leg of lamb, but I'm a bit short of money right now.' Mum took the biscuit tin where she kept her housekeeping money off the mantelpiece. 'I was sure I had three pounds in here at the start of the week.'

'Before the air-raid siren on Monday?' I asked.

'That's right.'

'And you left the door unlocked when you went to the shelter?' I asked.

'Of course. You're not going to get burglars going round in the blackout are you?'

'Aren't you?' I murmured.

'I must have taken it out to do a bit of shopping and dropped it in the street,' she said.

Half an hour later we were in the dining room eating a sort of stew with bits of lamb, carrot and rice. It tasted better than it looked, but I was that hungry I could have eaten the head raw, tongue and all.

'Mum, can I talk to Dad?' I asked.

'They won't let you into Firbeck air base. Why do you want to talk to him? He'll have a bit time off before Christmas, he reckons.'

Sally was just about to answer and give away our plan, so I cut in, 'I want to ask him about the police.

69

I want to write about the police for a project in school,'
I said.

'You find somebody that'll let you use their
telephone and I'll give you the number to call,' Mum
said.

Sally grinned. 'I know where there's a phone.
I know.'

'Where?' I asked.

She looked out of the window. 'Am I Sherlock
Holmes or Dr Watson?'

'Holmes,' I said.

'Am I Sexton Blake or Paula Dane?'

'Sexton Blake,' I said through my teeth.

'Does that make you Paula Dane?' my sister asked.

'If you like.'

'Then I'll tell you after tea tonight. . . Ma? What's
for tea?'

'Sheep's-head soup, of course.'

12

Over the English Channel
1 September 1940

Ernst Weiss sat at the controls of the Heinkel He 111 as it flew west towards the English Channel. There was no moon but enough starlight for them to see the coast and the water below as they crossed it.

The sky was empty. After a cloudless day and almost five hundred German bombers over England, the island sat in silence.

Ernst pushed his control stick forward. The plane headed for the dull, flat sea. It was low enough for the crew to see fishing boats being shaken and rocked as they passed over it. It was low enough to avoid the radar beams from the English coast.

'We are invisible,' Ernst chuckled, as white cliffs appeared five miles ahead. 'The English have a song, you know,' he said into his microphone. He began to sing quietly:

'There'll be bluebirds over
The white cliffs of Dover
Tomorrow, just you wait and see.
There'll be love and laughter
And peace ever after
Tomorrow, when the world is free.'

'What does it mean?' the gunner asked.

'It means there will be peace and freedom as soon as we have won the war,' he said.

At the last moment, he tugged back on the controls and the Heinkel soared over the white cliffs. 'Turn west twenty degrees,' the navigator said.

'I don't think we'll need you and the X-Gerat beam to find Biggin Hill airfield tonight,' Ernst laughed. 'After all the bombs that have fallen on it today, you'll be able to see it from the moon!' The pilot turned to the man who sat behind him in the cockpit. 'Ready? We'll be there in ten minutes.'

The man nodded. He tightened the straps on his parachute and picked up a suitcase. 'I've got the radio. Hope I don't smash the valves when I land.'

'Pistol?'

The passenger patted his jacket pocket, 'Yes, loaded and ready.'

'Passport?'

He patted another pocket. 'Tonight I am Swedish, but with a British Identity Card.'

The Heinkel skimmed over villages and farms, woods and railway lines. 'Some fine targets down there,' Ernst sighed. 'I wish we had a few bombs on board.'

On the horizon, he saw the orange glow of fires and a tall column of smoke in the calm evening air.

He lifted the nose of the plane and climbed. 'Get yourself back to the bomb bay. The bomb-aimer will tell you when it's time to jump.'

The passenger nodded, patted Ernst Weiss on the shoulder and walked to the rear door of the cabin.

'Passenger ready!' came a voice in the pilot's earphones.

'Fifty seconds to Biggin Hill,' the navigator's voice added.

'Bomb doors open,' Ernst said and felt the plane jerk as they did.

'Five seconds. . .'

'Best of luck . . . and jump!'

The pilot circled the plane and saw the parachute open as the German spy fell towards the flame-lit fields by the side of the airfield.

As the Heinkel passed back over the landing strip, they saw buildings burning and fighter planes smashed, deep craters in the runways and white arcs of water from a dozen fire engines.

Biggin Hill airfield, Kent, England
1 September 1940

The weary firefighters on the ground looked up in horror as they heard the engines of the Heinkel He 111 above them.

One of them looked up and shook his fist. 'There's nothing left to bomb, Jerry!' he cried. He waited for the explosion. There was the crackle of burning huts and the hiss of fire hoses. The men fell silent.

Another raised an arm and pointed. 'Parachute! They're sending in the paratroops.'

In the glare of the light, the firefighters strained their eyes. 'I can't see anything. How many were there?'

'Just one.'

'Can't be paratroops. It'll be a spy. They've dropped him to send back a report of the damage. If he radios back to say our airfield is finished, then they'll know they're winning. They can send the bombers again tomorrow and there won't be any Spitfires to welcome them.'

One of the airmen was struggling with his mechanics to pull his Spitfire away from the fuel tank in case the fire reached it and destroyed a good fighter plane. 'We'll have to get him then. Phone the Home Guard at Addington.'

'No phones, sir,' a mechanic said. 'They've all been wrecked.'

The pilot ran to the only hut that wasn't burning and came out with a pistol. 'One of you men, come with me,' he ordered.

'I'll come, Sergeant Henderson,' a young RAF driver said. 'We can take the supply wagon.'

'The group captain's car would be faster.'

'But some of the roads are damaged. The car would be wrecked if it hit one of those craters, sir. The supply wagon's got bigger wheels.'

'You're right,' Sergeant Henderson said as they headed towards the lorry. Take the masks off the headlamps,' he ordered.

The lorry's front lights had metal disks over them with just a narrow slot to let out the light.

'It's against the blackout laws, sir,' the driver argued.

'Oh, McCready,' the pilot laughed. 'The place is lit up like a bonfire beacon. One extra pair of headlamps isn't going to make any difference to the blackout – but it will help us see the spy.'

'We don't know where he landed, sir,' the driver said as he climbed into the cab and started the engine.

'The fireman was pointing to the west. They wouldn't be stupid enough to drop him too close, or we'd all have seen him – Jerry was just unlucky someone looked up and spotted him from Biggin Hill. And if they dropped him too far west they'd see him in Addington. No, he's somewhere between here and Addington. And what's between here and Addington?'

'Jewel's Wood, sir.'

'And if you were a spy landing in a strange country, where would you want to be dropped?'

'Near a wood, sir. I could hide the parachute and nobody would find it for weeks,' the driver said as he swung through the shattered gates of the airfield and turned west.

'Exactly. Mind the craters, but get there as fast as you can before Jerry has time to get his brain in gear. He won't be expecting *us*.'

The driver pressed his foot to the floor and the engine roared. The lorry bumped forward. 'He could head in any direction,' the driver said.

'No, he couldn't,' Sergeant Henderson said. 'He's come to report on the damage to Biggin Hill so he'll be coming this way. It would be too hard crossing the fields and the fences, dodging cattle. He'll be heading up this road, over Saltbox Hill.'

The lorry reached the top of the hill and the valley stretched out ahead of them. Three miles away, the village of Addington gave a glow in spite of the blackout. Jewel's Wood, just ahead of them, was black as a cave.

'Stop here,' Sergeant Henderson ordered.

'Shall I switch the engine and lights off so he doesn't see us?' the driver asked.

'No. If he's where I think he is, he'll have seen and heard us by now. Let him know we're after him. He'll be scared . . . and scared men make mistakes.'

They sat for a while with the only noise the clatter of the old engine. Moths fluttered around the headlamps and owls swooped over the fields. The hedges were thick enough to hide a man. The trees of Jewel's Wood could hide a small army.

Sergeant Henderson looked at his watch. 'Ten

minutes since he landed. Enough time to hide the parachute. Now he's in the wood. He's looking at us and wondering how long we're going to stay here. He will have forged identity papers – probably speak good English. Good enough to think he might get away if Home Guard patrols stop him.'

'How long do we wait?'

'Thirty seconds, McCready. He's just moved from the edge of the wood and onto the road.'

'I saw nothing! You have sharp eyes, sir.'

'That's why I'm a pilot, McCready. A pilot with bad eyes is a dead pilot. Now, he'll walk up to us, bold as brass, and try to bluff his way to Biggin Hill. He'll have a gun, so make sure you stay behind the headlamps at all times. The light will blind him, but step in front of the lamps and you'll make a perfect target.'

'Yes, sir,' McCready said, and there was a tremble in his voice.

13

The man walked up the road towards them, wearing a raincoat and a felt hat. He stopped and smiled when he reached the wagon. Sergeant Henderson and McCready stepped out, slammed the doors but stayed behind the headlamps. 'Halt!' the pilot shouted.

The man in the raincoat stopped and smiled. 'Good evening . . . well, not a good evening, I think.' He looked past the lorry to where the sky glowed orange behind the hilltop. 'Biggin Hill has taken a battering, I think.' He spoke good English, but with an accent.

Henderson shouted towards the rear of the vehicle. 'Ready, men? Keep your rifles aimed at his head.'

'Yes, sir,' McCready shouted back, playing the game. 'Keep that rifle up, Smith!' Then he changed his voice to answer his own order. 'Yes, sir.'

Henderson spoke firmly. 'Place the suitcase on the ground very carefully – we don't want to damage it.'

'Just a few clothes and some catalogues – I sell farm implements, to help England win the war,' the man explained. 'Dig for Victory.'

'We don't need German ploughs, thanks,' Henderson laughed.

'Not German. I am from Sweden, and Sweden is not in the war. Here, I can show you my papers,' the stranger cried and reached inside his coat.

'Stop!' the pilot shouted. 'I have six men with rifles

aimed at you. You may be able to shoot me, but you will be dead two seconds later. Reach slowly into your pocket and pull out the pistol you have hidden there. Hold it in your finger and thumb so I can see it.'

The man sighed and did as he was told. He held up a Luger pistol in the light of the headlamps.

'You use that to threaten the farmers who don't want your ploughs, do you, Fritz? Put it on the ground and take two steps back.'

The German spy obeyed. McCready stepped forward and gathered the gun from the road.

'So?' the spy asked. 'Now what? You shoot me?'

The pilot stepped forward and walked towards the German. 'No, Fritz, we do not shoot you. That is the Gestapo way. You are in Britain now. You will be given a fair trial. But first you will come to the Home Guard base at Addington with me. I have a little job for you.'

'If I refuse?'

'Ah, if you refuse, then I *will* shoot you.'

An hour later, McCready and Henderson were sitting in a chilly school hall that served as Addington's Home Guard base. The mix of ancient and boyish guards stared at the stranger the way you'd stare at a new type of poisonous toad – partly in fear, and partly in wonder. They kept their hands wrapped tightly around their old rifles.

'Now,' the pilot explained. 'This is the way it works. Tomorrow, officers from Special Operations will come from London to talk to you. They will offer you a deal, I expect – to send messages to Germany as if you have avoided capture. Special Operations will feed you lies, and you will pass on those lies to Mr Hitler and his friends.'

The German nodded wearily. 'And if I do that they will let me live?'

'I'll say! You'll be far too valuable to shoot!'

The spy took a deep breath. 'I am a loyal German, but I do not like Mr Hitler and his Nazi thugs. They are not worth dying for, my friend.'

Henderson nodded. 'That's good, because you can help me with a small problem *tonight*, my friend.'

Again the spy nodded. 'My spy masters will be expecting me to send a message. If I don't, they will get suspicious.'

'Exactly. So, you'll send them a message. You'll tell them that today's raid damaged two aircraft hangars, but they were empty as the Spitfires were on patrol. You'll tell them that one runway was damaged, but the other runway has been patched up. No fuel tanks were hit and telephone lines to the radar stations are working well. If they attack again tomorrow, then the squadron at Biggin Hill will blow them out of the sky.'

The German smiled. 'I can add that there will be a brass band waiting to welcome them if you like.'

Henderson shook his head. 'I hear the Nazis aren't very good at understanding jokes. Just send the message. Young McCready is fluent in German so if you try to trick us by sending anything else he will know. And old Bert over there – the one with a shotgun and a beard – is an expert on codes. He was head of the secret services for his army battalion in the last war. He will check your codes. Come here, Bert. Watch as our Jerry friend sends his message.'

'Yes, sir,' the old man said and hobbled across the dusty wooden floor.

The spy switched on the radio and after a series of whistles and screeches, he found the right waveband for sending a message. He wrote it out in English, then in German and then in code.

'All right, McCready?'

'Yes, sir.'

'All right, Bert?'

'All correct, sir.'

'Then send it.'

An hour later, the driver was grinding his way back up Saltbox Hill towards the ruined aerodrome. 'I can't speak German, you know, sergeant.'

Henderson laughed. 'I didn't think you could, and old Bert couldn't read a code book if you sent him back to school for twenty years. But our Jerry friend didn't know that.'

The driver changed gear as the lorry reached the top of the hill and they looked down on the shattered airfield. The fires were out, but oily smoke was drifting towards them and stinging their nostrils. McCready said, 'It's just as well he didn't speak to me in German. He just had to say something like, "Can I have a cup of tea?" and I wouldn't have understood. He'd have guessed we were lying. I was nearly wetting myself.'

Henderson shrugged. 'I don't think he was that bothered. He's out of the fighting now. He'll be better fed than he ever was back in Germany, and he'll probably live long past the end of the war.'

The driver let the lorry roll carefully down the cracked and cratered road towards the airfield.

'That's more than a lot of the lads at Biggin Hill will do. We can't take a lot more raids. Mr Churchill calls us "The Few", but the way Jerry shoots us down, we'll soon be "The Very Few".'

14

Sheffield, England
1 September 1940

'Ma,' Sally said after Sunday tea. 'Can I have a couple of pennies, please?' She looked like an angel. It was the face she put on when she wanted something.

'What for, Sal?'

'I want to give it to a poor lady down Attercliffe Road.'

Our mum sighed. 'You're a kind girl, Sal. I have a couple of pennies change from the milk bill,' she said and handed over two coppers.

'Thanks, Ma, she'll be really pleased.'

Sally nodded at me. 'Ready, Watson?'

'Yes, Sherlock.'

I grabbed my gas-mask case and followed Sally down the damp and darkening streets, as she pulled on her grey school coat and jammed her hat on her head. Her socks were falling round her ankles. She stopped to pull them up and I caught up with her. 'What poor lady wants tuppence?' I asked.

'You'll see.'

We reached the sweet shop on the corner and Sally stepped through the door just as old Mrs Haddock was pulling down the blackout blinds. The shop shelves were half empty and the wooden floor was dirty and greasy. The only sweets left inside the dusty jars were old and crusted. Battered boxes of candy cigarettes stood beside lollipops and gobstoppers that looked as though flies had been feasting on them. Fudge boxes were faded and the marshmallows were as shrivelled as Mrs Haddock's face. Glass jars that once held chocolates were empty, and the cinder toffee should have been called spider toffee. The shop smelled of sugar and dust.

'A packet of aniseed balls and a stick of liquorice,' Sally said.

'Have you got your coupons?' the woman asked as she shuffled behind the counter.

Sally pushed a scrap of pale-brown paper across the counter and the woman counted out a dozen aniseed balls into a bag. 'That'll be tuppence,' she said.

Sally reached into her pocket for the money. Mrs Haddock opened the till. 'I'll be glad to get to the bank when it opens tomorrow,' she said in her creaking voice. 'I don't like keeping all of Saturday and Sunday's takings in the shop.'

'You should get a safe,' Sally said.

'I've got one,' the woman said. 'But I didn't have time to put the money away after that air-raid warning on Monday.'

'Don't tell me,' I said. 'You were a pound short when you got back.'

'How did you know?'

'I guessed,' I muttered.

'Not only that, but I went to put my money away in the safe that night and the safe door was all scratched. It looked like someone had been trying to get in. There's some villains about. Can you imagine it? Robbed by your own neighbours.'

'How do you know it's your neighbours?' Sally asked.

'I don't mean me next-door neighbours. But it's someone that comes in the shop, regular like, and knows their way around. It could be *you*,' she snapped.

'We were in the shelter on Stanhope Street,' I said.

'Mebbe,' the woman said.

I looked around the cobwebbed shop that was lit by a dim lightbulb. 'You can't have that much in the safe,' I said clumsily.

'Can't I? Can't I?' she screeched. 'Are you calling me a pauper? Are you? Think I'm only fit for the workhouse, do you? Do you?' She picked up a broom and shook it at me.

Sally said, 'Sorry, Mrs Haddock, he's a bit thick,' before she dragged me into a corner and hissed, 'She makes a fortune. She gets chocolate on the black market and sells it from under the counter. There's people desperate to get their chops around some chocolate. No coupons but twice the usual price.'

'But this scruffy shop –'

'She keeps it scruffy so the trading inspectors don't come snooping. But half of Sheffield knows she sells chocolate. It's like she says, someone knows she'll have a safe full of money.'

'We should tell the police. I mean, the black market's wicked –'

'Aw, Billy Brainless! If Mrs Haddock stops selling chocolate, you'll be the most hated boy in Sheffield.'

'But how do you know all this?' I hissed.

'Everybody knows,' she said. 'All the girls in school know.'

It was always like that. Girls just *know* things boys don't. I never understood how.

'Where's the tuppence for them sweets? I haven't forgotten. I may be old, but I'm not potty yet.'

'There you go, Mrs Haddock,' my sister said. She handed over the money and walked out of the door into the drizzly evening.

I marched after her. 'Sally! You said you wanted money to give to an old lady!' I cried as she popped a sweet into her mouth.

'Mrs Haddock's an old lady, isn't she?'

'Yes, but –'

'And I gave her the two pence, didn't I?'

'I know, but –'

'So I was telling the truth, wasn't I?'

'Maybe, but –'

'So, let's go and do some detective work, and if you're really good, I *may* give you an aniseed ball,' she promised, popping the brown paper bag into her gas-mask box.

15

Sally refused to tell me where she was going, only that she knew where there was a phone we could use.

Eventually, we reached the end of Stanhope Street, where everything was black. 'The bomb shelter?' I laughed. 'There's no phone in the bomb shelter.'

Sally smiled her evil little tight-lipped smile. 'That's correct, Paula Dane.'

'Don't call me that.'

'Paula, Paula, Paula,' she said. 'What are you going to do about it?'

'Where is this phone?' I demanded.

Sally nodded to a brick building behind the shelter. It had a wall of sandbags piled up in front of the door to protect it from bomb blast and a thick roof of concrete slabs. I guess it was about the size of our school classroom.

'The wardens' post? Mr Crane won't let us use the wardens' telephone.'

'He will. Remember, we're going to help him – we're going to be his runners when the bombing starts, so he'll want to help us. You'll see,' Sally said and knocked on the door.

'Who's there? Friend or foe?' called Warden Crane.

'Sally and Billy Thomas.'

'Hang on . . . I'll turn out the light before I open the door –'

The door opened and the warden squinted into the darkness. 'Good evening, Warden Crane,' Sally said in her Sunday school voice.

'I had to turn out the light. If I'd left it on, I'd have to fine myself five shillings. Heh! Come in, come in.'

We stepped through the door and it closed behind us. The lights snapped on and we looked around the room. Hand pumps for fires hung from the walls and there were benches all around the sides. At the far end, there were a couple of beds and a man in a khaki uniform was toasting bread in front of an electric fire.

Warden Crane led the way into the room. 'Take a seat. This is Sergeant Proctor from the Home Guard. He often pops in here with the news.'

The Home Guard man was about thirty years old – young enough to be in the army. But when he turned to say hello, we saw he wore spectacles as thick as jam-jar bottoms. He was too short-sighted to fire a gun. 'Toast, anyone?' he asked.

He was spreading the bread with margarine. If we couldn't get any butter on the ration, Ma refused to buy that disgusting white grease. 'No thanks,' I said.

'You're all right, Mr Proctor, I've got some sweets,' Sally said. 'So, what news have you brought?'

'Well, it's not a secret – Mr Churchill was on the radio tonight,' the sergeant said. 'He said our bombers were flying to Germany right now and dropping bombs on Berlin. But he warned us that Mr Hitler will be angry. We all have to expect attacks any day or any night from now on.'

'"Cry 'Havoc', and let slip the dogs of war!"' Warden Crane cried suddenly.

'Did Mr Churchill say that?' I asked.

'No – William Shakespeare.'

'The one that's dead?' Sally asked.

'The very same,' Warden Crane nodded. 'Sheffield will be attacked soon.'

'And then you'll need us as runners,' Sally said.

'I think so,' he agreed.

'So will we be air-raid wardens?' Sally said slowly, looking as crafty as a dog with a sausage in its sights.

'You could say that.'

'So can we use the wardens' telephone, then?'

Crane looked at the Home Guard sergeant. 'Mr Proctor and I were just saying how we needed to get down to the Flying Horse on Tinsley Street –'

'The pub? You're going for a drink? I thought you were on duty,' I said.

The warden picked up his black helmet. 'We have had reports that the pub has holes in its blackout curtains. We need to check.'

Sergeant Proctor smirked. 'From the inside.'

Warden Crane spread his large hands. 'We will have to go inside to warn the landlord. If he offers us refreshment while we're there, it would be rude not to accept.' He raised an arm as if he were on stage.

Our headmaster did that when he spoke at the school assembly. '"The wine cup is the little silver well, where truth, if truth there be, doth dwell."'

The sergeant picked up his khaki helmet and an old Lee Enfield rifle – the sort they used in the last war, our dad said. 'So you kids can answer the telephone if it rings.'

'What should we say?' I asked, feeling my heart suddenly start to beat fast.

'We'll manage,' Sally said quickly. She turned to the two men. 'You go and enjoy your booze. We'll be fine.'

'You will,' the warden agreed. 'This is still a phoney war – nothing much is going to happen.'

'The phoney war ended tonight,' Sergeant Proctor reminded him. 'When our RAF lads dropped bombs on Germany.'

'Maybe,' Crane agreed. The men went to the door with the warden sighing, '"Give me a bowl of wine. In this I bury all unkindness."' He looked back at us. 'Put out the light . . . and then put on the light . . . once we're gone.'

A minute later, my sister and I were sitting at the wardens' table clutching the phone. 'Ready, Dr Watson?' Sally asked.

'Ready,' I said.

It took Firbeck a while to track down our dad. We had to wait at least ten minutes for the telephone operator to find him. I was pleased we weren't paying the phone bill.

'Is everything all right?' Dad asked, picking up the phone at last. 'What's happened? Is your mum all right?'

'Yes, everything at home's fine. Sally and me just wanted to ask you about police work,' I said.

'For a school project,' Sally shouted. I had the earpiece to my ear and Sally pressed her ear against it.

'It's a sort of story,' I said. 'A burglar that goes around in the blackout. There are two detectives trying to catch the thief –'

'Sherlock Holmes and Dr Watson,' Sally put in. She was really getting on my nerves.

'We want to make it real,' I explained. 'What would the police do if there was a burglar on the loose?'

Dad spoke slowly as he thought it through. 'You need to find a suspect. I mean, is there anyone in desperate need of money? Desperate enough to stay out on the streets when there could be bombs falling any minute. . . Well, they're either desperate or daft.'

'Thanks, Dad,' I said, making a note on a scrap of paper beside the telephone. 'What else?'

'Opportunity,' he said. 'Who has the *chance* to do the burglaries?'

'Anyone,' I said. 'People run for the shelters and leave their doors open. It would only take a few moments to pop into a house and steal some cash that's lying around.'

'Hmm! I'm not so sure about that. You'd be looking for someone in the shelters who's very chatty – talks to people about their money. You know the sort of thing – the thief will say, "Eeeeh, I've left my housekeeping on the table. I was counting it. I usually put it away at the back of the kitchen drawer. Do *you* have a safe place, Mrs Goodbody?" And they get the victim – Mrs Goodbody – to tell them.'

'So we go to the shelters and listen to people talking?' Sally asked.

'*Who* goes to the shelters?' Dad asked.

'The detectives in my story – Sherlock and Sexton,' I said.

'Right – yes, that's a good start. Of course, once you've got a suspect, you need to check they have an alibi,' Dad went on. 'Where was the suspect at the time of the crime? Of course, if they don't have a good alibi, it doesn't mean they're guilty. But if they *do* have an alibi, you can cross them off the list.'

'But how do you prove it?' I asked.

'Tricky,' Dad said. 'The police can take their fingerprints and see if there are prints at the scene of the crime to match. But that's no use if the thief wears gloves.'

'But Sherlock and Sexton can't do fingerprints,' I moaned.

'Then they'll have to call in the police. See?

These detectives are all very well in stories, but not in real life. Anyway, that's what's wrong with your story,' Dad added.

'What?' Sally asked.

'In real life, you would call in the police as soon as you were robbed,' he explained.

'Not for a pound,' I argued.

'A pound?'

'If you lost a pound, you wouldn't call in the police – you would just moan a bit,' Sally told him.

'And if it's just a pound, you may think you've dropped it in the street,' I said, remembering Mum's lost pound.

'No, no, no!' Dad laughed. 'Your story is getting daft now. We said the thief had to be desperate to risk his life when there are bombers on the way. Nobody risks their life for a quid. Ten pounds maybe. But not a one-pound note.'

'But what if they went around and took one pound from ten different houses?' I asked.

The line went quiet apart from a hum and a crackle. At last Dad spoke. 'That would be a clever thief,' he said. 'Oh, very clever. Steal ten pounds from Mrs Smith or Jones and they'd make a fuss, call in the police and catch you. But steal one pound from ten houses –'

'You still end up with ten pounds, but nobody would call in the police,' I put in.

'Yes, that's what a clever thief would do. Do you have many air-raid warnings?'

'About one a week, but the bombers never come.'

'Yet,' Dad said. 'One day they will and then our burglar could catch it. Of course – here's an idea for your story – the clever burglar might *know* the air raid is a false alarm!'

'How?' Sally asked.

'I don't know, but there may be some way you can call the Home Guard, say there are enemy bombers on the way and get them to sound the sirens. Everyone will rush to the shelters, but you know it's safe to wander the streets because you gave the false alarm.'

'I'll see if that's possible,' I said and made a note of that, too.

'If the burglar's that clever,' Sally said, tugging the telephone from my hand, 'our detectives will never catch them.'

'Ah, that's possible. Not every crime is solved, you know,' Dad admitted. 'So long as they don't get greedy and try to steal too much – that's how a lot of thieves get caught. Greed. But your thief may not be greedy.'

'Trying to rob a safe is greedy,' I said.

'That's big-time crime,' Dad said. 'A different class of villain. They play for big money and they fight dirty. Even Sherlock would have to watch out then.'

'Watch out?' Sally said.

'Watch out for knives and coshes and even guns. . . Those Home Guards have a lot of guns lying around. The sort of thief that would rob a safe would use a gun to protect his cash. Sherlock would end up with a hole in his head. No, make your story about a clever criminal who steals the odd pound here and there.'

'But we won't *catch* him at it!' Sally groaned.

'Then your detectives would have to set a trap – that's what I'd do. Get some money and put a secret mark on it. Make sure everybody knows where it is and the next time there's an air raid, you can check who's spending the marked notes.'

'Thanks, Dad,' I said.

We chatted a little longer about his work at Firbeck and the fighter planes that flew from there. Sally promised to show him the school project when he came home in December and we put the phone down.

'We don't have a school project,' I told her.

'Then you'll have to write it, Billy, won't you?'

I really hoped this Sherlock would end up with that hole in the head.

16

Biggin Hill airfield, Kent, England
2 September 1940

The spy sat at a table in the wing commander's office at Biggin Hill. The Special Operations officer from London looked at him. 'You did a good job last night, sending back a fake message.'

The spy shrugged. 'If I help you, then you let me live.'

The British officer smiled. 'We have lots of work for you, but there's one thing you can tell us now.'

'If I can, I will,' the German smiled.

'Your bombers hit their targets in the dark. We have a blackout, but it doesn't seem to do us much good. How do they find the targets?'

It was not a question, it was an order.

The spy swallowed hard and twisted his fingers. 'It is one of Germany's greatest secrets,' he whispered.

The officer spread his hands. 'Not really. We already know you have some sort of beam to guide your bombers. Every time you use it we learn more about it.' He leaned forward and spoke quietly. 'Here is a British secret. In two weeks, we will have cracked the secret of your beam. Tell us what you know and you won't betray Germany – you'll just make the war two weeks shorter.'

The spy rested his chin on his chest for a long while. Finally he looked up.

'You are talking about the X-Gerat radio-beam system. I trained with the Luftwaffe, so it's something I know about.'

'And now you can train us?'

The spy nodded slowly. 'I will.'

Dachau, Germany
2 September 1940

Manfred slept badly. Some nights he lay awake, listening for the British bombers to come and kill him. Other nights he had dark dreams about slaving in a bomb factory with the Polish girl sweeping up behind him. Then a kapo would march up to him and make him stand in a pool of freezing water till he collapsed, face down, and began to drown. That's when he woke, sweating and afraid.

In the morning, he dressed and wandered wearily downstairs. There was a rattle at the letterbox and his mother came in with a handful of letters. 'Here's one from Ernst at the aerodrome... Oh, and look, Manfred – he's written one to you, too.'

Manfred was suddenly awake. He took the letter and tore it open. He read it quickly and then read it again slowly. '*My dearest brother*,' it said, '*I am *delighted to tell you we are winning this war and I am safe and well. I was so angry to hear about our grandfather. I guess he will be out of hospital soon. He is as tough as the meat in our stew! Anyway, I told my commander about the British dropping a bomb on a harmless old man and how they are bringing terror to my family.'*

'What does he say?' Manfred's mother asked, looking up from her own letter.

Manfred covered the letter and thought quickly. 'Ernst says his commander wants to show the people of Dachau that there is nothing to worry about. He says that I can go to their bomber base and see how mighty the Luftwaffe is. Then I can come back and tell all the boys at school how we are going to win the war.'

'Oh, Manfred, that is wonderful. You can see all the planes you dream about. Maybe Ernst will even take you on a flight! Will you go by train?'

'Ernst says the bombs from the Dachau factory are delivered to his base once a month. I can take a ride on one of the wagons, and it can bring me back later.'

'That makes sense,' his mother agreed.

Manfred nodded. 'And Ernst says I can take a friend.'

'Little Hansl?'

'Maybe,' the boy said quietly. An idea was forming in his mind. An impossible, crazy idea. He jumped to his feet and slipped the letter into his pocket. 'I'm off to school,' he said.

The old clock ticked on the wall. 'You're half an hour too early!' his mother gasped. 'I've never seen you leave the house at this time.'

'I have things to do,' Manfred said as he snatched his coat and cap from the clothes-stand, grabbed his school bag from behind the door, and ran out into the street.

When he reached the end of the road, he turned and ran towards Hansl's house. He hammered at the door till his friend answered.

'Hansl, come quickly, I have a plan.'

'I haven't finished my breakfast.'

'Does it taste nice?'

'Terrible.'

'Then come on – walk up to the munitions factory with me and I'll tell you my news.'

Hansl grabbed his school stuff and followed Manfred down the road. The first leaves of autumn were falling and the hillside forests were turning gold and pale green. The hedge at the side of the road was full of ripe blackberries. The boys picked some and ate them. The bushes would soon be stripped by the folk of Dachau.

High above, the clear sky was scarred with the white vapour trails of aeroplanes, but it was still hard to believe there was a war on.

Manfred stopped and pointed at the factory. 'What I'm going to tell you is so secret, Hansl, we could both be shot if you say one word.'

'Shot?' the small boy said, and his eyes flicked around as if a sniper were hiding behind the hedge.

'Swear on the life of Adolf Hitler that you will tell no one what I say.'

'I swear on the life of Adolf Hitler that I will tell no one what you say.'

Manfred licked his lips and began. 'I want to get into the factory to write on one of the bombs.'

'I know that.'

'I know a way into the factory.'

'Is that the secret?'

'No – shut up.'

'Sorry.'

'That skinny girl we rescued from the bullies will get us inside the factory, but it will have to be on a night when one of the friendly guards is on Gate C,' he explained.

'Why?'

'Why what?'

'Why would she do that?' Hansl asked.

'That's the great secret,' his friend hissed. 'She wants to escape. If we help her to escape, then she'll get us into the factory.'

'Help a prisoner escape!' Hansl cried, and Manfred wrapped a hand around his mouth.

'Hush! Do you want the Gestapo to hear you in Berlin?'

'Mmmmf!' Hansl said shaking his head. Manfred released his smothering grip.

'Yes, Hansl. Helping a Polish prisoner to escape will get you executed. But this girl is no danger to Germany. If we help her get away, it won't mean we lose the war. My brother Ernst says we are already winning the war.'

'How will you help her?'

Manfred pushed a fat blackberry into his mouth and chewed on it as he turned back along the path to the town. 'I don't want to tell you now. But one day, I will come to you and ask you to do something for me.'

'What?'

'I can't tell you just yet. But if you promise to help with my escape plan, I'll get my brother to take you up in one of his planes after the war. You've always wanted to do that, haven't you?'

Hansl's eyes shone. 'Always, Manfred. But won't it be dangerous, what you want me to do?'

'Just a little,' Manfred said. 'But you have to trust me.'

'I do,' Hansl nodded.

17

16 September 1940

It was a fortnight before Manfred had a chance to put his plan into action. He didn't see the girl on the streets after school. He wondered if she was still alive.

Then, in mid-September, when the trees were half bare and leaves were whipping down the street, he saw her leave the grocery store and ran after her.

'Irena?'

She turned. He had thought she was icicle thin when he'd last seen her. Now she was even thinner and her dark eyes more sunken. She looked at him silently.

'I've been looking for you.'

'They changed my work. I sweep the factory by day and I have a new job most nights.'

'What's that?'

She fell silent and stared at the pavement, a strange look of shame and disgust on her face. 'People in the camp . . . slaves . . . they die.'

'And?'

'They are buried in a pit . . . but first their clothes are removed.' The girl looked ill. 'Suits, dresses, shirts . . . underclothes. Some are good material . . . some are rags. The good clothes are washed and given to German people. The rough clothes, with the lice and the stains, are washed and given to slaves. The rags are used for cleaning.'

'And your job?'

'I sort out the clothes into the good, the bad and the rags,' she said.

'The clothes off dead people? That's awful.'

She shrugged. 'It means I have something good to sleep on. Last night, I had a dead woman's fur coat to keep me warm. The dead don't mind. Some of the clothes have blood on them, but not many. The worst thing is –' She stopped and looked up at the evening sky.

'Yes?'

'There are more,' she said simply.

'More what?'

Irena looked at him as if he was simple. 'More than there used to be.'

'You mean it's harder work for you?'

For the first time, he saw anger in the girl's face. 'No, you German fool,' she spat. 'I mean there are more slaves dying. At first it was a few, but now they're getting weaker and the kapos are getting crueller. Now the burial pits are filling up. And most of them are Poles like me. One day I will join them.' She gave a small snort. 'I suppose the Germans will ask me to sort my own clothes before I die.'

'You won't die,' Manfred said.

She looked at him steadily. 'We all die.'

'I mean, you won't die in the camp. I have a plan. A plan for you to escape.'

'Where would I go?' she asked.

People in the street were looking at them curiously. The well-dressed schoolboy in a warm coat and scarf and the ragged slave girl. Manfred pulled Irena into an alley between the shops. 'You wanted to go to England,' he said.

She gave a small smile. 'When the war started, the Germans took over the radio stations. When we listened to the news, we only heard German lies. So my father found a way to get the BBC radio from England.'

'So you heard English lies instead?' Manfred said, scowling. 'If we listen to English radio, we will be shot.'

Irena went on as if she hadn't heard him. 'After the news there was music. There was a woman they call Vera Lynn – she sings beautiful English songs. We learned to speak English from the radio, and I learned to sing her songs.'

The girl wandered down the shadowy alley towards the rubbish bins at the back of the shops. Her thin voice rose into the air, sweet as an evening nightingale.

'There'll always be an England
While there's a country lane,
Wherever there's a cottage small
Beside a field of grain.

There'll always be an England
While there's a busy street,
Wherever there's a turning wheel,
A million marching feet.'

She stopped and looked east towards England.

'I think I can get you there,' Manfred said. 'But first you must help me get inside the factory.'

'Where do you live?' Irena asked suddenly.

Manfred explained where his house was.

The girl pulled a square of blue silk from a pocket in her dress. 'Silk. It belonged to a rich Pole who ended up in the camp.'

'Dead?'

'Of course. How do you think I got her handkerchief? If the Germans knew I had it, they would beat me.'

'Then why keep it?'

'Because it is beautiful,' she said simply. 'When it is a good night for you to visit the factory, I will tie this handkerchief to your front gate. You will come that night, to Gate C at ten o'clock. Do you understand?'

Manfred nodded. Irena turned away. The boy called after her, 'There'll always be an England,' and she gave him a half smile. 'There'll always be an England . . . even if it is ruled by Germany,' he murmured quietly to himself.

Manfred wrote to his brother to set the plan in motion. He asked Ernst if he could visit him at the aerodrome and if he could get a fake permit that would allow him to visit the factory. Amazingly, it arrived soon after. Now all he needed was a sign from Irena.

The weeks slipped by. The days grew shorter. The evenings came quicker, but every night Manfred looked for the blue handkerchief before he went to bed.

It didn't appear.

He sat with his mother and listened to the radio. It was cold enough now to light a fire but Manfred's mother only used a few pieces of precious coal and some scraps of wood she picked up from the bombed houses.

'We could be burning Grandpa's house,' she chuckled.

In late September, Ernst Weiss wrote to say Manfred's trip to the aerodrome must be forgotten for a while. Every day, his bombers were attacking England.

'We bomb their air bases by daylight. Their Spitfires shoot down a few of us, but many get through. Soon they will have no air bases left and no planes. Then we can invade England and the war will end. It may be over before Christmas.'

At the end of the month, Grandpa left hospital and came to live with them.

'Ha!' he cried one wind-whipped night when the gale outside sucked sparks up the chimney. 'Italy and

Japan have joined us in this war. It's as good as over. The British cannot hold on much longer.'

'Will Japan send troops to attack Britain?' Manfred asked.

'No, boy. Japan will use its mighty power to control the Pacific Ocean. If the Americans even think about joining Britain in the war, then Japan will conquer America from the west. Easy!'

Manfred nodded. If the war was going to be so short, he would have to hurry with his plan to set Irena free.

But still the blue handkerchief didn't appear.

October

18

Sheffield, England
16 October 1940

School was as dull as the October skies. In history lessons, old Mr Cutter taught us about the Battle of Hastings and the Battle of Stamford Bridge.

Mr Cutter was a chalk-dusted, Hitler-moustached, elbow-patched, blotch-faced, watery-eyed, stained-tooth man. He hated the way I wrote.

'Thomas, you cannot throw all those words together. You will never make a writer. You must write the way your English teacher tells you, in clear sentences.'

'But you understand what I mean.'

'That is not the point. You must write correctly.'

'Why?'

'Because . . . because I say so. Now, where was I?'

'At the Battle of Hastings,' Freddy York reminded him.

'Yes . . . the Battle of Hastings took place on the 14th of October, in the year 1066. That's 874 years ago yesterday. Or was it the day before yesterday? Anyway, it was the last time Britain was invaded,' he droned on like a wasp in a jar.

I didn't want to know about the *last* invasion.

Why couldn't we talk about the Battle of Britain? That's what they were calling the fight in the skies over England. I wanted to know what would happen the *next* time Britain was invaded.

Mr Hitler was sending his bombers over every night to kill the people in London. As soon as the RAF was destroyed, the German troops would sail across the English Channel and take over the country. Our fighter pilots were trying to shoot them down with their Hurricanes and Spitfires. They were holding back the swarms of Luftwaffe planes, Dad said, but only just.

Sheffield was safe and there hadn't been any air-raid sirens lately, so we couldn't try out our burglar-catching plan.

I waited for Sally at the school gates and we raced home till we had no breath left to hear the latest news.

'Has Mr Hitler landed in London yet?' Sally panted.

Our mum was listening to the radio and waiting for the four o'clock news. 'Not yet, Sally. Let's pray he doesn't or we'll all end up speaking German.'

'I can't speak German,' Sally cried. 'What'll I do?'

'You'll have to learn,' Ma said with a shrug. 'You'll have German teachers in your school.'

'Will they be as nasty as our Mrs Morrison?' Sally asked.

'Nastier . . . Nazi-er!' I laughed.

'Nobody's as nasty as Mrs Morrison. She gave

Mary Ramsbotham the cane yesterday and the cane snapped she hit her that hard. But then she just got a new cane out and kept on hitting her. Mary didn't cry though. We watched. She said she wasn't going to cry and she didn't. I think that made Mrs Morrison hit her harder and –'

'Hush, Sally,' Mum said. 'I want to listen to the news.'

We sat at the kitchen table with a glass of milk and some dripping on bread. The news was a shock. The biggest attack of the war hit London last night, the man on the radio said. Four hundred enemy aircraft bombed for six hours. The RAF sent forty fighters against them, but only shot down one enemy plane.

'They can't shoot down the enemy at night,' Ma muttered.

'The searchlights show them where the German planes are,' I argued. I'd seen the searchlights sweeping the Sheffield clouds when the false alarms came.

'The searchlights don't light up bombers that are flying over twelve thousand feet – that's what the fighter pilots at Firbeck tell your dad. Now, shush – what was that he said?'

'He said the Germans attacked Birmingham and Bristol last night as well,' Sally told her.

'The war's getting closer,' Ma whispered. 'Maybe it's time we sent you two away to the country.'

'No-o!' Sally and I cried together.

'Where's Birmingham?' my sister asked.

'Just a quarter of an hour away in an aeroplane. They make the Spitfires and Hurricanes there. If they're attacking Birmingham, it won't be long before Sheffield gets its own Blitz.'

'Why's that?' I asked.

Our mum snapped off the radio. 'The Germans know what our factories make. Hadfields makes the shells, Vickers makes the Spitfire engines . . . then there's the steelworks and the coalmines. We're sitting in the middle of a firework waiting for somebody to light the fuse.'

She picked up our empty mugs and plates and carried them into the kitchen. Sally's eyes were bright. 'There'll be an air-raid warning tonight,' she said softly.

'What?'

'Listen, Dr Watson. The Blackout Burglar knows the whole of Sheffield is waiting for a raid. So, he'll send a message to the Home Guard saying there's an attack on the way. The sirens will sound. People will run for the shelters. The Blackout Burglar'll rob them. If he's clever, he'll take a little from each house. Or he'll look for one big pile of money – like Mrs Haddock's safe, or the fortune Mrs Grimley says she's got hidden away.'

I hadn't thought of that. Sally acted stupid most of the time. But her brain was as sharp as broken glass.

'So, what can we do to catch him or her?'

Sally chewed her lip and thought. 'We'll be no use in the shelter. We need to be out on the streets, looking for anybody wandering around. We'll follow them. See if they go into houses. Then, when the all-clear sounds, see where they go home.'

I thought about it. 'What if there really is a raid? Mum says we're next. What if bombs start falling? We'll be caught in the open.'

'Smart question, Dr Watson. We need to know if there really is a raid.'

'I just said that. So what would happen if German planes were heading for Sheffield?' I asked.

'Somebody would phone and warn the Home Guard,' she told me.

'Who? Who would phone?' I asked.

Sally screwed up her eyes and thought. 'Dad told us, didn't he? Before he left. The air force has ray guns –'

'Not ray guns,' I sneered. '*Radar*. Some sort of radio signal that bounces off enemy planes and lets us know they're coming from fifty miles away.'

Sally nodded. 'Radar – ray gun – anyway, they phone and let the Sheffield Home Guard know.'

'No,' I said. 'No, Sherlock, they don't. They phone the RAF fighter bases. They get our Spitfires and Hurricanes up in the air and shoot the bombers down before they can do any damage!'

I went to the cupboard by the fire where Ma kept old newspapers to burn. I pulled some out and found the one I wanted. 'Look. August. The Germans sent planes to attack the south of England. They thought all our fighters would head south and leave the north without any planes. So they sent hundreds of bombers to bomb the north. The radar saw them coming and our fighters shot them down over the sea.'

'So they never even reached England?' Sally asked.

I read the report. 'A dozen houses in Sunderland were wrecked, but that's about all. The radar saved the north-east.'

My sister shook her head. 'I don't see how that helps us, Watson.'

Now it was my turn to feel clever. I took a plate and put it in the middle of the table. 'That's Sheffield.'

'It's a bit white,' Sally sniffed.

I put the saltcellar a few inches away. 'That's the RAF fighter base.'

Near the edge of the table I put the pepper pot. 'That's the radar station.'

I quickly folded a sheet of newspaper into a paper plane. 'German bomber.'

'You won't get many bombs in that.'

'The edge of the table is the coast. Radar sees the bomber. What do they do?'

Sally tapped the plate. 'Phone Sheffield.'

'No!' I cried and pointed to the saltcellar. 'They

phone the RAF.' I picked up the pepper pot and flew it towards the paper plane, making machine-gun sounds. I let the bomber drop. 'See?'

Sally screwed up her face so hard she looked like one of the evil gnomes in her book of fairytales. 'The RAF will know about the attack before we do.'

'Yes.'

'RAF bases like Firbeck?'

'Yes.'

'So when we hear the air-raid siren go off, we phone Dad. We ask him if the fighters have taken off.'

'Uh-huh, that's right.'

'If they have taken off, then the raid is real and we head for the shelter.'

I grinned. 'And if the fighters are on the *ground*, it's a false alarm.'

'We can stay out of the shelter and look out for the Blackout Burglar –'

'And be safe. The burglar thinks he's the only one who knows it's a false alarm. But so will we!'

Sally's eyes went wide. 'That's quite clever, Dr Watson.'

'No, it's not. It's *brilliant*. Let's go out and help Warden Crane,' I said, grabbing my coat and scarf and gas mask from the peg on the back of the door. 'As soon as the siren goes, we'll run to the wardens' post and phone Dad – the wardens will all be out getting people into the shelters.'

Sally found her hat and coat and gloves and called, 'We're off to help the warden, Mum!'

'What if there's a raid?' Mum called back.

'Don't worry. We'll use the nearest shelter,' Sally said as she slipped out of the door after me into the moon-bright streets.

I looked up. 'It's a bomber's moon, all right.'

19

Dachau, Germany
16 October 1940

Hansl was moaning as the boys tramped home from school. 'Manfred, you said you were going to get inside the factory and write on a bomb. You said you'd arrange it.'

'I know, Hansl. And I will.'

'Yes, but you've been saying that for weeks. The war will be over before Christmas and you'll never get to kill a Tommy. We've invaded Romania now – where's Romania, Manfred?'

'Oh, somewhere down near Italy, I think.'

'So why have we invaded Romania?'

Manfred turned up his coat collar against the chill wind that blew from Russia in the north-east. He thought of the girl in her thin grey dress and hoped she hadn't had to stand in a freezing lake like her father. 'Grandpa says Romania has lots of oilfields. Now we've captured them, we'll have all the petrol we need for our planes and tanks. We'll smash Britain from the air and march across to Russia in our tanks.'

'How do you march in a tank?' Hansl asked.

'You know what I mean. Anyway, invading Romania is a smart move. Mr Hitler knows what he's doing.'

They turned into Manfred's street. 'So when are we going to the factory?'

Manfred stopped and looked at his small friend. 'Tonight, Hansl. Meet me at the gate to our back garden at quarter to ten tonight.'

'Really?' Hansl cried.

'Really,' Manfred said, 'and bring some sausage.'

'Sausage?'

'Everybody knows your mother is a friend of the butcher's wife. She can get as much sausage as she likes without a ration card. Bring some with you – nice and fresh, mind. Two packets.'

Manfred watched Hansl race off down the street. He took a step towards his front gate and carefully untied the blue handkerchief. He slipped it into his pocket and walked into the house.

That night, the boys ran through the green-lit streets, stopping at every corner to look out for police patrols. Sometimes, they met groups wandering from the taverns, grumbling about the food and drink, remembering how good it had been before the war.

Manfred hurried past the new houses that were being built on the spot where Grandpa's house had been bombed. Ahead, he saw the factory, looming in the light of the moon. 'If the British knew it was here,' Manfred said, 'they'd bomb it tonight when the moon is full.'

Hansl just nodded and stared at the grim building. From the road he could hear the thumping of machinery and the rumbling of trucks. Light spilled out through the blackout screens and showed the shadows of bent workers trudging wearily around the concrete building. They pulled trolleys with heavy crates towards the waiting trucks. Small cranes lifted the crates gently onto the back of the lorries.

'Bullets and bombs,' Manfred said.

When they reached the gate, the friendly old guard was on duty. 'The little girl said you'd be here,' he said.

'So can we go in?'

'No, no, no, no, no – it's not that simple,' the man said. He wiped a drop of water from the end of his nose. 'First I have to look after myself – I need some sort of note from you. Then if the Gestapo check, I can say you had permission.'

'The Gestapo!' Hansl squeaked. 'The Gestapo torture people, don't they? The boys in school say they rip out your fingernails to get you to talk. They fasten wires to you and give you electric shocks. They're Mr Hitler's Secret Police. I didn't know they were here!'

'No, no, no, no, no,' the old guard sighed. 'The Gestapo run Dachau camp – they supply the slaves to work in the factory. The factory pays the Gestapo for the slaves' work.'

'So who pays the slaves?' Hansl asked.

Manfred groaned, 'No one, dummy. That's why they're slaves. They get fed, they get a place to sleep and they get clothes when they wear out. But they don't get money. They're prisoners and traitors.'

'Ah,' Hansl said. 'So what do the Gestapo do?'

'They just come along from time to time to check. If a slave looks too weak to work, they take him back to the camp and fetch a fresh slave,' the guard explained.

'And the sick slave gets a rest?' Hansl said.

The old man shuffled his feet and sniffed away another water drop from his nose. 'Something like that.'

Manfred handed the man the note from his brother. 'Will this do?'

The guard flicked a torch over the paper and saw the Luftwaffe aerodrome address printed at the top. 'That'll do.'

'So can we go in now?'

'No, no, no, no, no. Even with the note, I am taking a risk. If a Gestapo officer turns up, he may still want to know what I'm doing letting two kids wander round. No, no, no, no, no. I need paying if I'm going to let you in.'

'I don't have any money,' Hansl said with a sigh.

'Sausage,' Manfred hissed. 'Remember?'

'Ah, yes!' Hansl cried. He turned to the guard. 'I have two hundred grams of fresh sausage here.'

'Let me see it.'

Hansl unwrapped the greasy paper and the spicy scent of the sausage drifted up on the chill east wind.

'Ahhhh!' the guard groaned. 'Beautiful. Bring me that and you can come in any time, boys.' He lowered his rifle, took the wrapped sausage and said, 'Little Irena's waiting for you by the side door on the left. Watch out for the trucks. They can flatten you thinner than a slug under a jackboot.'

The boys ran through the gate in the wire fence and up the path to the factory. There was no chance of being run over by a truck because even in the darkness the roar of their engines gave them plenty of warning.

But the car that came up behind them was ghostly quiet. The first they knew it was there was when its harsh horn sounded behind them. The huge Mercedes screeched to a halt. The rear door opened and a tall man stepped out, waving a pistol at them. He tilted his head back and looked down his eagle nose at them. 'Get out of my way, Polish scum. Next time I will order my driver to run you down. He only stopped because he thought your under-human bodies would damage the car. Move!'

Manfred dragged the frozen Hansl onto the thin grass at the side of the road and watched the man get back into the car. His throat was too dry to speak. At last he managed to say, 'Gestapo . . . a Gauführer . . . a commander for the region. Very high up.'

'How do you know?' Hansl whispered as the car wheels spun and it shot past them.

'Two stripes on his armband,' Manfred explained.

'What does he want? I thought the Gestapo didn't come here very often? Maybe we should go straight home,' Hansl moaned.

'No. If he didn't shoot us now, he must have more important things to worry about. We should be safe.'

They hurried up the road and reached the side door where Irena waited, hopping from foot to foot. 'The Gestapo have arrived,' she said. 'We must be careful. Come in quickly.'

20

Manfred and Hansl followed Irena through two doors and were met by the roar of machinery. The light was dazzling after the dim moonlight outside. Rows of workbenches had screeching lathes and steel saws, mechanical hammers and conveyor belts. Hundreds of grey-faced, silent men were bent over the machines. Others wandered down the aisles, sweeping up the metal shavings or mopping up oil drips with rags.

The tall figure of the Gauführer marched down one of the rows, led by a scuttling kapo. The Gestapo chief's badges sparkled in the light – badges that showed a shining silver skull on his black uniform.

The kapo stopped and pointed at one of the workers. The man had a shaved head and he looked as if he had been powerful and heavy at one time. Now his clothes hung on him like a scarecrow. He switched off the machine and turned to face the Gestapo chief. The Gauführer shouted something that Manfred couldn't hear over the sound of the other machines. The slave looked up angrily and seemed to argue. Suddenly, the Gestapo chief's arm swung and struck the slave's face with the back of his hand. In the same movement, he reached for the pistol in a holster under his leather coat.

The slave jumped behind his machine then began to run down the aisles. The Gauführer raised his gun and fired. Workers dived under their machines as the escaping man began to weave between them.

He headed straight for the door where Manfred, Hansl and Irena stood. His face was white and his eyes bulged like a panicking horse. Another bullet splintered into the door an instant after he'd stepped through it. Manfred felt the hot air as it passed his ear.

The Gestapo chief ran past them, shouting at his guards to make sure the main gates were all shut, then he hurried out into the night.

Manfred heard three more cracks of the pistol. A minute later, the Gauführer stepped back through the door and spoke to the kapo. 'That is one less troublemaker for you to worry about. He asked for more food, did he?'

'Yes, Gauführer Linz.'

The Gestapo chief began to reload his pistol and smiled a thin smile. 'When I was at school we read an English book by a man called Dickens. It was called *Oliver Twist*. A boy in the book asked for more food.'

'Yes, Gauführer Linz. Did they shoot him?'

'No, but they should have done. These under-humans should be grateful we feed them at all. In fact, to teach them a lesson, you will not let any of them eat for the next day.'

'Then they may not be strong enough to work tomorrow,' the kapo said.

'Good. The weakest ones will fail – get rid of them and replace them. We have just taken some Romanian gypsies prisoner. Nearly a hundred. They are fresh and strong. You can set them to work tomorrow.'

'Yes, Gauführer Linz,' the kapo said, bowing as the Gestapo chief strutted out through the door.

Manfred was silent and Hansl had tears in his eyes. Irena's face was blank.

'Will they starve *you* till you're too weak to work? Even though you had nothing to do with it?' Manfred finally asked.

'I don't need much food – not like the men who do the heavy work.'

Hansl slid a hand inside his jacket and pulled out a second packet of sausage. 'This will keep you going.'

Irena looked at the meat. 'I will give it to the ones who need it,' she said, and quickly hid it under a pile of old clothes in a room to the side of the factory.

The workers were slowly getting back to their tasks, more weary than ever, barely shocked by the murder of their comrade.

'You want to see the finished bombs?' the girl said.

Hansl nodded and followed Irena across the factory floor and into another room. It was as large as an aircraft hangar and filled with metal racks holding bombs and crates. They were wheeled in from the factory at one end and loaded onto the waiting trucks at the other.

Irena ran to a small room at the side, filled a kettle from a tap and placed it on a gas ring to boil. She put tea into a pot and got a cup ready.

'I thought we were going to write on a bomb,' Hansl said.

'I have a job to do. I must make tea for the kapo or I will be beaten. And if you want to touch the bombs, the kapo must be in a good mood.'

She turned back to her work and carried a mug of steaming tea into the loading room. The kapo was better fed than the other workers and there was a cruel look on his narrow, unshaven face. 'You're late, girl,' he snarled and raised a stick.

Manfred stepped between the man and the girl. 'It's not her fault. The Gestapo came to arrest a worker and he was shot. We had to hide from the bullets.'

'Who was shot?'

'Nicolaus Piłsudski,' Irena said.

'Serves him right,' the kapo told her. 'He was always a troublemaker. I thought I heard something. It's hard to tell with the noise of the machines. Another one dead, eh? And who are you? You don't look like workers.'

'We're from the town,' Manfred explained. 'My grandpa is a hero from the last war. He asked me to write on a bomb with chalk, and now we need your help.'

'Why should I help?'

'Hansl can get you food – his mother has friends in the butcher's shop.'

The man gave a smile showing crooked, yellow

teeth. 'For good food you can write on my forehead with a carving knife.'

'We want to write on one of the bombs that are headed for my brother's base, at Cambrai,' Manfred explained.

The kapo shrugged and walked towards a list that was pinned to the wall. 'Cambrai is supplied on the tenth of each month. The October run was last week. Try again in November, and don't forget the food!'

Irena led the way back through the factory to the door. A pile of clothes was lying there. The girl picked up the jacket. There were blood-stained bullet holes in the back. A German guard stood over them. 'Get them sorted, girl, it's your job.'

'Yes, sir,' Irena muttered.

'Whose are they?' Manfred asked.

'Nicolaus Piłsudski's,' she replied.

'But he was shot just ten minutes ago!' Manfred gasped.

'Yes. This is a factory of death. People as well as bombs pass in and out. It's all the same,' she said, and began to pick through the clothes.

Manfred and Hansl walked back to the gate in silence. They collected Ernst Weiss's letter from the guard. 'Get what you wanted, lads?' the old man asked.

The boys shook their heads and walked back to the town in the light of Manfred's blue-bulb torch. They were as silent as the stones beneath their feet.

21

Sheffield, England
16 October 1940

We met Mr Crane on the corner of Whitworth Lane.
'Need any runners, Mr Crane?' I asked.

'I need some extra eyes,' he said.

'Mum cooked a sheep's head last month,' I said.
'I could have saved you the eyes if I'd known you
wanted some.'

'I *mean*,' he said in his voice as rich as cream,
'I need eyes in sensible heads to look out for people
breaking the blackout rules. Mr Jobling from District
72 is sick, so I have to cover his streets as well.
We can't afford to let one chink of light out tonight.'

'Because there's a bomber's moon,' Sally put in.

'Indeed, my child. I have a feeling in my bones
there will be a raid,' he said.

'I had the same feeling,' Sally nodded. 'Didn't I,
Billy?'

'Tell us which streets to go to, and we'll do them
for you,' I said.

The warden pulled out a map and showed us the
area he wanted us to cover. 'Pay particular attention
to the back alleys,' he warned us. 'People are careful
about the front rooms because the neighbours can see
the light and warn one another. But they get careless

about the kitchens at the back. They think the back wall hides the light.'

'It does,' Sally said. 'Especially when you're little like me and can't see over the wall.'

'A German bomber can see over the back wall,' the warden reminded us. 'Don't be afraid to open back gates to check.'

'And if the siren sounds?' I asked.

'Head for the nearest shelter. See – it'll be here,' he said and pointed to the map.

'What if the bombers come before we get there?'

'Stay away from buildings. Find an open space and lie flat on the ground. The blast should pass over you.'

'What if a bomb lands on me head?' Sally squeaked.

'You won't know much about it,' the man chuckled.

'If you're scared, I'll help Mr Crane by myself,' I jeered.

'I'm not scared, Billy Thomas. I'm just checking what to do. Let's go.'

We set off down the road for District 72. The last trams were running, packed with people on their way home from work. There were a few cars on the road driven by posh people who had enough petrol coupons. They had masks over their headlights with just a small slit to let out light to see where they were going. But they couldn't see people crossing the roads, and people couldn't see them.

Just the week before, Mum had told us about

a woman who was knocked over and killed in the blackout. 'Daft ha'porth was wearing a black coat!' she had sighed. 'They tell you to wear something white – a scarf or something – and men to let their shirt tails out of their trousers. You can't blame the drivers.'

I kept Sally on the pavement as much as I could and looked extra carefully when we had to cross the road. The pig-bins with stale food stank, so we knew when we were near a street corner.

There weren't many people on the streets once the trams and buses had stopped running. Dogs trotted around in packs of three or four. Some growled at us. Sally growled back and they ran off. Cats watched from safe perches on the top of back yard walls. Their eyes glowed green like traffic lights. We entered the moon-washed alley behind Bakery Lane.

'I think that's a light,' Sally said.

I lifted the latch and pushed the door that led into the alley. To the right was the shed that served as a toilet. The yard was cluttered with an old bicycle, a dustbin, a pig pail full of rotting food scraps, a few flower pots and a Morrison shelter that was waiting to be taken into the house and assembled. That was what I tripped over, sending some of the steel pieces clattering onto the concrete.

'Who's there?' cried a frightened voice behind me. I spun round and Sally clung to my arm. Someone was in the toilet hut. 'Who's there, I said.'

'Nobody,' Sally answered.

'Yes, there is. I warn you, I have the toilet chain in my hand. I'll thrash you with it if you don't get out of my yard.'

'You'll not be able to flush the toilet then,' Sally called.

'I'll flush the toilet *first* and come after you next. Just wait till I pull me pants up.'

It sounded like it was an old man. Sally and I began to tiptoe towards the back gate. Then we heard a sound that made us freeze. The man pulled the chain and the toilet flushed. We heard the chain being unfastened from the toilet cistern and the door was thrown open. The man had a fierce grey moustache the size of a yard brush, and he looked as scared as us.

'Aaargh!' he cried when he saw us.

'Aaargh!' Sally and I cried and backed up against the old bike.

'I said I'd thrash you – and I've got a dog in the house. A big German Shepherd dog.'

'They call them Alsatians now, mister,' Sally said.

'Never mind the name,' the old man shouted. 'His teeth are just as sharp whatever you call him.'

'What do you call him?' I asked.

'Eh?'

'His name? We had a dog called Goofy, like in the Mickey Mouse films at the Tivoli.'

'Erm . . . I, er . . . I call him . . . er . . . Rover,' the man said. 'I call him Rover.'

'I don't believe you,' Sally said.

'You'll believe me when he sinks his choppers into your skinny little backside,' the man argued. 'I keep him to guard against burglars like you.'

'We're not burglars, we're air-raid wardens,' Sally said.

'There's been a lot of robberies when the air-raid siren sounds,' the man said.

'We know,' Sally said.

'And you look a bit young to be wardens. Anyway, I know our warden – Mr Jobling. I went to school with him and his brother.'

'Mr Jobling's sick,' I said. 'We're helping Mr Crane from the Attercliffe district.'

'A likely story. I'm going to call the police,' he said and edged his way towards his back door.

'Have you got a telephone?' Sally asked.

'Yes, I *have*,' the man said proudly. 'The only one in the street.' The chain glinted in the light of the moon as he made his way towards the kitchen door.

Sally sensed the man's fear and stepped forward boldly. 'Good! Go on. Call the police. And while you're on, give yourself up.'

'What for?'

'Showing a light after blackout,' she said and pointed to the open kitchen door. 'If you report us, then we'll report you.'

'Awwww!' the man moaned. 'I only went to the toilet. I was only going to be a minute.'

I guessed what Mr Crane would have said if he'd been there, and I said it. 'It only takes a minute for a German bomber to fly over and see it.'

'What German bomber?' The old man asked and squinted up into the moonlight.

At that moment the low wail of the siren began. '*That* German bomber!' Sally cried.

'Ohhhh! I wish I had that shelter built,' the old man groaned.

'You'll have to get to the public shelter.'

'I'm going,' the man said. He reached behind the kitchen door to grab an overcoat, pulled it on and slammed the door behind him.

Over the noise of the siren, we could hear people shouting all the way down the street. Shoes clattered down the lane, dogs barked with the sudden excitement.

'We have to get to the wardens' post,' I said. 'Call Dad. See if it really is a raid. Hurry. We're a long way from Stanhope Street.'

The moon shone on Sally's grin. 'We don't need to go anywhere. You forgot, Dr Watson, there's a telephone just inside this house.'

Don't you just hate it when someone is right *all* the time?

22

We pushed open the kitchen door. The old man's house smelled of stale food and musty carpets. He'd left the light on and we blinked in the glare.

'There's no dog,' Sally said.

'That's right, Sherlock. I knew there wouldn't be.'

The telephone was in the hall. I picked it up and dialled 100.

'Operator here. How may I help you?'

I asked to be put through to Firbeck air base and waited as the connections clicked and buzzed.

'Firbeck!' a bored woman's voice said on the other end of the line.

'Can I speak to Sergeant Eric Thomas in the military police?' I asked.

'Who are you?' the voice asked. 'He's probably on patrol around the fence. Is it urgent?'

'That depends,' I said. 'I'm his son. I live in Sheffield. The air-raid siren's just gone off,' I explained and held out the telephone so she could hear it. 'Dad said to call when it went off to find out if there really is a raid.'

'Why?'

'Ah . . . ah . . .'

Sally had been doing her usual listening trick and snatched the receiver from me. 'Our mum is very sick. The doctor says if we move her, it could kill her.

We only want to get her into a shelter if we really, really have to.'

'Sick? What's wrong with her?'

Sally looked blank for a moment. I took the phone back. 'Tuberculosis,' I lied. 'She's coughing blood all over the place.'

'Sorry to hear that, son. But don't worry, you can let your mum stay where she is. If there was a raid, our Hurricanes would have been up in the air ten minutes before your siren sounded. Tell your mum it's another false alarm.'

'Thank you, I will,' I said.

'And give her my best wishes,' the woman said.

'Thanks.'

'And I'll let Sergeant Thomas know his wife's very sick, could even be dying if she's coughing blood, poor love.'

'No!' Sally and I cried together. 'I mean, Mum doesn't want Dad to worry – she's been bad like this before. So long as she rests, she'll be fine,' I said.

'If you're sure –'

'Very, very sure,' I said.

'Then you take care. And if you want to give me your number, I can give you a call if there ever is a real raid?'

'No! We'll phone you – we don't want Mum upset by the telephone ringing. We don't get many calls – she'll think it's bad news about Dad –'

Sally snatched the telephone. 'Just one ring could kill her!' she said and gave a little sob.

'If you're sure . . .' the woman repeated.

'Yes, thank you,' Sally snivelled. 'Thank you, and God bless,' she added and put down the receiver.

'Poor Mum,' I said. 'Are you going to mop up the blood or do I have to do it as usual?'

'Very funny, Dr Watson,' she snapped, 'but we have a job to do. Let's get back to Attercliffe and see who's on the streets when they should be in the shelter.'

We hurried back through the kitchen and out of the yard into the alley. The streets were silent again. Even the siren had stopped. A chill wind from the hills whistled through the electricity wires and blew dust around the street corners into our faces.

'Stay in the shadows and make a note of who's walking about,' I told Sally.

'How do I make a note?' she asked.

'I brought a paper and pencil from school specially,' I reminded her. 'It's in your gas-mask case.'

'Yes, but if I'm in the shadows, how do I make a note?'

My sister had to be the most awkward girl in Yorkshire. 'You can make a note in your head, Sherlock. We'll write a list when we get back home.'

'When's that?'

'As soon as the all clear sounds.'

'Where do we start?' she asked.

'Let's go to the places the burglar's been before. You take Jubilee Terrace and I'll watch Mrs Haddock's sweet shop. If he's got away with it once, he might try again.'

Sally nodded and we headed back towards the familiar streets near our home. Mrs Haddock's corner shop was at the end of a parade, so I had plenty of shop doorways to choose from. I left Sally to walk on to Mrs Grimley's lane and backed into the deep doorway of the ironmonger's shop, which was a few doors down from the sweet shop.

A dog scared the life out of me when it came sniffing at my shoes. 'Push off,' I hissed. Luckily, it wagged its tail and ran away.

In the silence, I could hear the distant rumble from the steelworks. Then there was the rattle of a car engine. I pressed my back against the shop door so its weak headlights didn't catch me. When it reached the corner, it stopped. The car door opened and a man stepped out. He wore a heavy overcoat and a hat with a wide brim that hid his face. He looked around as if he was afraid of being seen, then he disappeared to the far side of his car and I heard the door open. The man pulled out a heavy box. He carried it to the sweet shop and put it on the ground, then he tapped on the window. Soon after, the shop door swung open. There were a few muffled words and then he vanished inside.

I felt as if I'd been holding my breath for five

minutes. I kept my eyes on the shop door and stepped out into the street. I ran up and looked at the front of the car. It was a Lanchester fourteen – a six-cylinder model with overhead valves and water-cooled engine. I could write down the notes later. But there was something about it that made me think I'd seen it before. I looked at the number plate and tried to keep it in my head: CU 3127.

That's when I heard the sweet shop door open again. I threw myself into the doorway of the baker's next door. But now that dog was back and heading straight for me. I started to panic, but at the last moment it smelled the sweet shop and sat on the pavement, looking up at Mrs Haddock.

If the man *was* the burglar, he'd most likely throw me in front of the car, run me over and drive on. That's what I'd do if I was him. I'd look just like another blackout road accident. I suddenly found I needed the toilet. I heard him speaking quietly and then he stepped into the moonlight and raised his hat politely. I saw his face clearly for a moment. And that's when it all came together – the car, the voice and the face.

'Goodnight, Mrs Haddock. I'll be in touch as soon as I can get more supplies,' he said. 'It's always a pleasure doing business with you, madam.'

'It would be when you charge three times the price I paid before the war.'

'Supply and demand, madam. It's something

they call supply and demand. If you don't want the chocolate, I'll sell it to someone who does. Maybe someone who'll pay me more again!' he chuckled.

The man was doing a black-market deal with the sweet-shop owner. But he wasn't a dealer in sweets . . . well, not usually. He was a teacher. He was *my* teacher – Mr Cutter. I'd once seen him drive by in that car. I asked Mum how a teacher could afford a £350 car. Now I knew.

23

My history teacher walked around the front of the car so he didn't pass my useless hiding place. He started the engine and drove off.

Mrs Haddock watched him go down the street. '"Supply and demand, madam",' she spat. 'Stuck up twerp.' Then she walked back into her shop.

I hung around. There was still a chance the burglar would try again – he wouldn't know Mrs Haddock was staying late to take in her fresh supplies. But the all-clear siren sounded and the streets began to fill with people going home from the shelters, grumbling about the latest false alarm.

'I'm staying in the house next time,' a young woman complained.

'And you can be sure *that'll* be the one that's not a false alarm,' her friend said.

Sally was home before me, and I reached the front door at the same time as Mum. 'You're safe then. You found a shelter in time?' she asked.

'Yes, Mum,' I lied.

'Another false alarm. I'm wondering if it's worth dashing to the shelter. May as well stay at home nice and warm when the next alarm goes off.'

'And you can be sure *that'll* be the one that's not a false alarm,' I said wisely.

She gave me an odd sort of look and offered to

make us a cup of cocoa while I poked at the dusty coal fire and tried to get warm again.

While Mum went into the kitchen to make the cocoa, I told Sally about seeing Mr Cutter at the shop. 'Do you think I should report them?' I asked.

'No point. Everybody does a bit of black-market dealing. There was a fire down at a warehouse the other week and Mrs Gibson's husband is a firefighter. He rescued two dozen tins of peaches. She's been selling them a shilling a can.'

'That's against the law,' I said.

Sally sniffed. 'You didn't seem to mind when you scoffed them last Sunday.'

I shook my head. Sally seemed to know more about things that went on in the city than I ever did. 'So what did *you* see, Sherlock?' I asked.

'Something very interesting,' my sister told me. She lowered her voice so Mum couldn't hear us. 'Just as I turned into the lane, I saw a woman come out of the house next to Mrs Grimley's. She had a scarf over her head and it was dark, of course, but she looked like she was up to no good. She was weird. A huge nose sticking out the front of her headscarf.'

'Weird?'

'Her dress went right down to her ankles, and she was really tall, for a woman.'

'A headscarf?'

'Yes, except more like a hood.'

'It wasn't a woman. It was a man in a hood,' I said.

'Ha!' Sally snorted. 'What man is going to walk around Sheffield in a dress?'

'He calls it a cassock,' I said. 'You saw the vicar, with his cowl up.'

Sally nodded slowly. 'Well done, Dr Watson.'

'Did he see you?' I asked.

'Of course not. I was in the shadows just like we agreed. Anyway, I went down to Mrs Grimley's back gate, into her yard, and sat in the toilet.'

'You did what?'

'It's all right. It's really clean. She keeps it nice and she has real toilet paper –'

'Yes, but why the toilet?' I hissed.

'Because it's warm, of course. *And* you can look straight out to her back door if you leave the door open a crack. You can even sit on the toilet and be comfy –'

'Never mind that. What did you see?'

'I'm coming to that. I heard a noise – it was a rattle on her dustbin lid. I think it was rats trying to get into her dustbin. Then there was a scuffle and I think that was a cat trying to chase the rat.'

I rubbed my eyes. 'Sally, are you going to tell me what you saw or do I have to hit you over the head with the poker?'

'Mum would be cross if you did that, you bully.'

'Only if I bent the poker. Get on with the story.'

'The back door opened – it creaked like the cry of a lonely ghost, begging to be set free from a dark dungeon.'

'Eh?'

Sally scowled and screwed up her small face. 'I am telling you a story. Our teacher says you have to do lots of describing to get the reader in the mood.'

'I'm in the mood to use that poker on you.'

'I heard footsteps creeping silently down the path –'

'How could you hear them if they were silent?'

'I have the ears of a bat.'

'Yeah, well the bat wants them back.'

'I looked out and saw the back of a large man. He tried the door of Mrs Grimley's kitchen. It was open. He looked inside. Then he closed it and walked back down the yard to the alley.'

'Who was it?'

'I'm coming to that. It's dark in that yard and he had a helmet on so I couldn't see his face. There was only one thing to do – brave little Sally Thomas crept out of her safe toilet and followed the stranger into the dark alley. I looked out and couldn't see which way he'd gone,' she said.

'Didn't your bat's ears tell you?' I asked.

'The all clear was sounding. I walked to the end of the alley, where it turns into Attercliffe Road, and *bang*! I walked straight into him! I screamed.'

'What did he do?'

'He screamed an' all!' she said. '"What are you doing out in an air raid?" he asked me. "What are *you* doing out in an air raid?" I asked him back. "It's me job," he says. And do you know who it was?'

'Winston Churchill?'

'Stop being daft.'

'Adolf Hitler?'

Sally looked at me sourly. 'It was Sergeant Proctor from Dad's Army.'

'The Home Guard?' I said. 'Then he's right. There's no reason why he shouldn't be on the streets.'

'He looked at me through those jam-jar glasses and, if you ask me, he looked very suspicious. As if I'd caught him doing something sneaky. Anyway, he *says* to me it was his job. And I says, "I thought I saw you going into Mrs Grimley's yard." And he says, "Yes. We need to know every house in every street in our area. That way, when the bombs fall, we know just where to look for survivors."'

'That's the job of Mr Crane and the ARP wardens,' I muttered. 'The Home Guard have to guard the factories, canals and railways when the Germans drop men on parachutes.'

'That's what I thought,' Sally said. She took the paper from her gas-mask box and spread it on the table. At the top she wrote 'Suspects'. She said, 'I reckon Sergeant Proctor goes at the top of the list –

we said the Home Guard could be the ones setting off the false alarms. How do you spell sergeant?'

'S-a-r-j-e-n-t,' I told her.

'Vicar Treadwell at two, Mr Cutter your teacher at three and Mrs Haddock at the sweetshop at four.'

I nodded. 'They all knew it would be safe to stay out of the shelter. Even if they weren't thieving tonight, they must know something the rest of us don't.'

'Should we tell the police?' I said.

'They'll laugh,' Sally said. 'When Dad was in the police, he kept going on about getting stuff that showed the villains had done it.'

'Evidence,' I said.

'Evidence. We'll get evidence.'

I was just going to ask Sherlock how she planned to do that when there was a heavy knocking at the front door. Mum hurried from the kitchen to answer it. We heard her say, 'Oh! There's nothing wrong, is there? It's not my husband is it?'

A deep voice said something to calm her down and finished, 'your kids.'

'You'd better come in, Constable Anderson,' she said and led the way into the living room. We looked up to see a grey-haired old policeman taking off his helmet and looking down on us.

'Good evening,' he said. 'I've come about the Blackout Burglaries.'

Sally jumped to her feet and waved her scrap of

paper at him. 'I have a list of four people we think could have done it,' she said.

The grey eyebrows lifted in surprise. 'And I have a list of *two* people the police suspect,' he said. 'Shall we see how our lists compare?'

Sally reeled off the four names. 'Well?' she said. 'What are the two names you have?'

He opened his notebook. Mum stood with her back to the fire, chewing at her nails. Sherlock didn't see it coming, but I did, just a moment before he looked up at us. 'The names I have here are . . . Billy and Sally Thomas.'

November

24

Dachau, Germany
10 November 1940

When the first snows came to the hills around Dachau, the boys at the school were happy. They threw snowballs until the school bell rang, and built a snowman in the shape of Herr Gruber, their teacher, and turned the pavements into deadly slides.

Manfred and Hansl didn't join in.

'Irena,' Hansl said, blinking away the stinging snow as he looked across the fields towards the munitions factory.

'I know,' Manfred said. 'She'll be cold.'

'I could take her an old coat,' the smaller boy said.

'The kapos would notice straightaway. They'd take it off her. Maybe even beat her. She said she sleeps among the old clothes, so she should be warm enough.'

'The clothes of dead people.'

'I know,' Manfred said again as they walked into the classroom, stamping their feet on the mat at the door.

'But we can take her extra food tonight,' Hansl said. 'I've been collecting some to bribe that kapo. Tonight's the night for the Cambrai lorry.'

'We can't keep her alive for ever,' Manfred muttered.

'Just till the end of the war. It will be over by Christmas.'

'No,' Manfred sighed. 'It won't.'

'What won't?' Herr Gruber said, walking in behind them.

'The war won't be over by Christmas, sir.'

The teacher's face turned red with rage and he began shouting. 'Stand at the front of the class, Weiss. Now class 7, sit at your desks. Sit still and listen to this!'

The boys hurried to their seats and in seconds were sitting silent and straight. The teacher breathed heavily and began to speak in a voice as sharp as vinegar. 'This boy says the war will not be over soon. Herr Hitler says we are winning the war. The newspapers and the radio say we are winning the war. But this traitor here thinks he knows better, isn't that right, Weiss?'

'I just said it may go on longer than we thought. My grandpa was in the last war. He said it was just the same. They thought it would be short, but it lasted over four years.'

'That was then, this is now,' the teacher raged. 'If Herr Hitler says we will win soon, we will win. First, you will be caned as a lesson to all the boys in the class – hold out your hands.'

Manfred stretched out his hands in front of him while Herr Gruber brought his stick down savagely six times on each hand. Manfred didn't cry out, but he bit his lip and couldn't stop tears forming in his eyes.

'Second, you will be reported to the police and a policeman will visit your house this evening to make sure your parents never repeat those lies again.' The teacher sent a boy with a message to the police station and the class carried on with their lessons.

After school, Manfred and Hansl trudged home through the slushy pavements. 'The munitions factory tonight?' Hansl asked when they reached the street corner where they parted.

Manfred looked at the large, grey Mercedes parked outside his house. A soldier sat in the driver's seat, stiff and hard-faced. 'I don't think so, Hansl. I don't think so.'

'But the girl?'

'It can't be helped. Not tonight. See you tomorrow . . . I hope.'

Inside the house, his grandpa and mother stood by the window. In front of the fire was a man in a black leather coat with silver skull badges and two stripes on his arm band. His nose was as sharp and curved as an eagle's beak.

'This is Gauführer Linz,' Mrs Weiss said.

Manfred almost said, 'I know,' before he bit his tongue and stayed silent.

The Gestapo chief stepped forward with a thin smile on his face. 'You are Manfred.'

'Yes, sir.'

'Herr Gruber will have told you that we cannot have people going around spreading stories about Germany's defeat. We want to hear of nothing but victory. Understand?'

'Yes, sir.'

'And what should we do with boys who tell tales of defeat?'

'Shoot them, sir?'

Gauführer Linz laughed softly. 'If we shot you, we would not have enough Hitler Youth to grow up and fight for the Fatherland. Well, not if we shot you without a little warning. But your brother is in the Luftwaffe and he knows we are winning the war in the air –'

Manfred was about to open his mouth to tell Gauführer Linz that Ernst had said they were losing the battle in the skies over England. He caught sight of his mother's eyes flashing a message of fear. 'My brother says we are winning the war in the air.'

'And your father is serving with the army, and he can tell you we are winning the war on land.'

The last letter from his father had said that the invasion of Greece was going badly and the Greeks were putting up a brave fight in the mountains where German tanks couldn't crush them. This time it was Grandpa's turn to widen his eyes in panic.

'My father says we are winning the war in Greece,' Manfred lied.

'Your grandfather is a hero from the last war, Manfred. You come from a true German family. It would be a shame to shoot you,' Gauführer Linz said and stepped closer so the boy could smell the brandy on his breath. 'I think you made a mistake. You said something foolish.'

'I did, sir,' Manfred said.

'So we will mark it on your record. We will not punish you. Your teacher, Herr Gruber, has already done that.'

Manfred's hands were still sore. 'Yes, sir.'

'Herr Hitler is a kind man. He would not want to see you punished again. But we must all work together to bring victory. Remember one of our favourite Hitler Youth songs?'

Manfred's mind went blank with fear and he struggled to recite the words:

'You, Führer, are our commander!
Make us one, form us into
An iron chain, man beside man.
Into a wall of loyalty around you.'

The Gauführer nodded. 'An iron chain, Manfred. You must be a link in the chain. If you turn out to be a weak link, then we will have to remove you. Understand?'

'Yes, sir.'

'Good. Then we will leave it at that.' Gauführer Linz reached inside his jacket and pulled out his

150

pistol. 'Make one more mistake and I will shoot you myself. Do not make me do it, Manfred. It would upset your mother, your father, your grandfather and your brother. Imagine the disgrace it would bring – they would not be able to walk down the streets of Dachau if the whole town knows the Weiss had a traitor in the family.'

The man put his pistol back in his pocket and walked to the door. 'I'll see you out, sir,' Mrs Weiss said.

Manfred felt faint and chilly even in the glow of the fire. 'Oh, Manfred,' his grandpa muttered. 'Learn your lesson. Never speak of defeat. Even if the Russians and the British are standing at the gates of Dachau, you must say that we are winning.'

'I only said –'

'I don't want to hear, boy. Watch your step. Go to Hitler Youth meetings and sing the songs, do the exercises, and watch your tongue. Now, get to your room. There'll be no supper for you tonight.'

'Yes, Grandpa.'

'Oh, and Manfred, I know about your escape route from your window. Do not try it or I will call Gauführer Linz to find out where you have gone and why.'

Manfred swallowed hard. 'Yes, Grandpa.'

25

Manfred sat in his room and began to write a letter on a page from an old school book. It took him a long time, but at last he was satisfied with his work and made a neat copy on a plain sheet of drawing paper. He read it to himself:

'*Dear Ernst,*

I hope you are well and still dropping lots of bombs. It has been snowing hard here. Thank you for your letter which allowed Hansl and me to enter the munitions factory. We have missed this month's delivery to you at Cambrai but hope to try again next month. It would be wonderful if we could travel with the bombs to your airfield. When you were home, you came to our school and met our teacher, Herr Gruber. He has asked if you would let us inspect a bomber and report back to the class. If you did this, he would give me top marks in the winter exams and our mother would be so proud. Please write and say we can visit you on 10 December. Stay safe.

Your loving brother,
Manfred.'

The boy sealed the letter in an envelope. Next morning he would ask his mother to put it inside her own letter to Ernst.

The guard at Gate C of the munitions factory huddled

deep inside his hut at the gate. The girl asked him the time for the fifth time.

'Ten-thirty,' he told her. 'You had better get back – the kapo will be wanting his tea. This cold spell has killed quite a few of you under-humans in the gravel pits. There'll be a lot of clothes for you to sort.'

'If the boys come –' she said.

'I will send them up to the side door. But they won't be coming now. Not at this time. Not in this weather.'

'They wouldn't let me down,' Irena said.

'Everybody lets you down in the end,' the man replied.

The girl turned and ran up the snow-covered road. Slaves had been sent to clear the path a dozen times that day, but each time the winds from the mountains swept it back again. The bomb-delivery lorries slithered out and struggled along the roads with their endless cargo of destruction.

When Irena reached the factory, it was quiet. The machines had been turned off. Some crackled and creaked as they cooled. The workers were heading for the large loading room. 'What's happening?' she asked one of them.

'We have been called to a meeting,' the man muttered.

When they arrived inside the crowded room, Irena saw her kapo and Gauführer Linz standing on a crate so they could look over the heads of the silent, shuffling workers.

The kapo cried, 'Workers, we are honoured to have Gauführer Linz with us here tonight. The Gauführer has come from a meeting with Herr Hitler himself and has some wonderful news for us.'

Gauführer Linz tilted back his head as if the smell of the workers disgusted him. 'Herr Hitler says we are close to winning this war. The air raids on England must increase. Their bombers have dared to attack our cities and we shall have revenge by wiping their cities from the face of the Earth!'

He waited as if he expected the workers to cheer, but hundreds of empty eyes gazed back at him. Waiting.

'Herr Hitler has looked at the records from his factories,' the Gauführer went on. His mouth turned down and a red spot appeared on each cheek. 'Some factories are not producing the munitions fast enough.' He took a deep breath as if the next words were hard to say. 'Dachau is not producing enough.'

At last a worker spoke. 'What more can we do?'

The Gauführer glared at the workers. 'A factory in my district. Failing. Remember what it says on the gates of the camp: "Work and you shall be set free". At this rate, you shall never be set free.'

'We work till we drop dead!' someone muttered. 'Maybe he wants the corpses to start making bombs?'

'Hush, he'll hear you,' a friend said, 'and you'll be joining the corpses.'

But the Gestapo chief was too angry to hear anything but his own fury. 'I do not like to fail. So I have a plan. We will fill this factory with the fittest and the strongest. Your kapo here has drawn up a list of the feeble and sick workers who are letting me down. These weaklings will be sent to another camp.'

'To die,' someone near Irena murmured.

But the Gauführer was saying, 'They will be given easier work – sewing uniforms for our magnificent armies, growing food for the great German people, caring for the sick under-humans and burying the ones who don't survive.'

'Death camps,' a voice whispered. 'I have heard the Nazis are creating death camps. The enemies of Germany go there and never come out alive.'

Gauführer Linz said, 'Your kapo here has a list of the names of the workers who will go to an easier life in another camp. We are arranging the transport. You will leave here on December tenth. Kapo?'

The work master stepped forward with a list. He began to read each name slowly, looking up to check that the worker had heard. One by one, slaves heard their name and closed their eyes, defeated.

'And finally,' the kapo said, 'Irena Karski.' His eyes met the girl's and he gave a cruel smile.

Gauführer Linz looked at him. 'A girl? Her name wasn't on the list.'

'I just added it,' the kapo explained. 'I was expecting

my tea tonight and it didn't arrive. She needs to go to
. . . an easier life.'

The Gauführer shrugged. 'Fine. I will sign the
list.' He took a pen from his leather coat and, in just a
moment, signed away a hundred lives.

'Be ready to leave a month from now. And
remember – "Work and you shall be set free".'

The Gestapo chief marched out and the kapo said,
'What are you waiting for? Get back to your machines.
You are idle. A disgrace to Germany. In your last
month at Dachau you will work harder than you ever
thought possible, or I will beat you till my arm aches.
Now move.'

The next day saw the wind change to the south-west
and the snow begin to thaw. Manfred was trudging
home through slush when he heard his name called.
Irena was standing at the corner of the alley by the
side of the grocery store.

'You didn't come last night.'

'I was being punished,' he said and quickly told
her about the visit of Gauführer Linz. 'Maybe next
month.'

'My last day. On tenth December, they will send
me to another camp.'

'A better camp?'

'The workers say it is a death camp,' she said
quietly.

'No!' Manfred gasped. 'The German people would never kill a harmless girl – not even an under-human! It's a lie.'

Irena shrugged her thin shoulders, said, 'So it's a lie,' and turned away.

'No. Wait!' Manfred called. 'I have a plan. On tenth December, I'll get you away. Trust me. I won't let you down.'

She looked at him with empty eyes. 'Perhaps,' she said and walked away.

December

26

Dachau, Germany
10 December 1940

Manfred stepped out into the hazy moonlight. This time there had been no need for him to sneak out through his window. His brother Ernst had written a letter to their mother, telling her Manfred was invited to visit him at the airfield. His mother had fretted and complained, but Grandpa told her Manfred was a growing boy and the trip would do him good. He'd learn far more than he ever would in school.

Mrs Weiss gave in and made sure Manfred had a couple of meals packed for the trip. 'Shall I come with you to the factory and see you safe onto the truck?' she asked.

But Grandpa cut in. 'For goodness' sake, no! You'll show the boy up – having his mummy holding his hand and waving him off. He's a young man. My mother didn't wave me off when I marched away to the trenches in 1916. No, no. Say goodbye at the front door, then let him make his own way there.'

Manfred nodded. 'Hansl's coming, too. I'll be fine.'

The wind was dry but icy as Manfred and Hansl hurried through the streets of Dachau after the curfew.

The moon was almost full and, on the road to the munitions factory, they felt as if it was lighting them like a searchlight.

'This is great, Manfred,' Hansl whispered. 'A real adventure.'

But Manfred felt nothing but fear. If his plan didn't work, Irena would be sent off to another camp to die. He had planned this as carefully as he could, but he knew there were a dozen things that could go wrong – and most of those would end up in death for himself as well as Irena. He never told Hansl what the real plan was.

The old man stood at the gate, but tonight it was busier than ever. Not only were the lorries arriving and leaving loaded with crates of bombs, but trucks with canvas hoods on the back arrived with fresh workers from distant camps. Manfred saw bleak faces look out from the back of one lorry; sunken eyes full of wonder, empty of hope. Then, moments later, another lorry crackled through the iced puddles full of the old workers who were being sent away. This time the eyes were empty of life. They were the eyes of men who were so far down the road to death they looked as if they were already there.

'Hurry, Hansl,' Manfred moaned.

'What's happening?'

'They're changing the workers and bringing in new ones. Irena will be sent off before we get there.'

Manfred handed the note from his brother to the old guard at Gate C. 'Haven't I seen this note before?' he asked.

'Yes,' Manfred said nervously. 'We need to return to finish our school report.'

'I can't let you in,' the guard said.

'Why not? You have a note,' Hansl argued.

'I have a note, but I don't have the magic password,' the guard said and smiled a toothless smile. 'Last time, I had something else. . .' He raised his hand to his mouth and gave a mime of sucking food between his gums.

'I have sausage,' Hansl said.

'Sausage!' the guard cackled. 'The magic password.'

Hansl reached inside the pocket of his coat and pulled out two packets. He unwrapped one and took out a piece of dry bread with a thick slice of sausage in the middle. He passed the sausage to the guard, who quickly pushed it into the pocket of his greatcoat.

'Pass, friend,' the old man chuckled and raised the barrier to let them through.

As they walked on the frozen grass at the side of the road, Hansl asked, 'Why do we have two packets of food with us, Manfred?'

Manfred sighed. 'I won't be going back with you tonight, Hansl – I'm going with the bombs to Cambrai to visit my brother.'

'Can I come, too?' Hansl clapped his small hands.

'No. I'm sorry. I never promised you that. Remember, your reward will be a flight in my brother's plane *after* the war.'

'Awwww, Manfred!'

'But you can do a very, very brave thing,' Manfred said. They were close to the factory now and Manfred headed for the side door where the clothes-sorting room stood.

The factory was not as noisy as it had been. Many machines were turned off so the old workers could show the new workers how they were operated. The clothes room stank of sour sweat and worse.

Irena was waiting inside. When the boys entered the room, she jumped to her feet. First, she handed a pair of scissors to Manfred. 'Cut off my hair so I look like a boy,' she said quietly.

Hansl watched, open-mouthed, as Manfred obeyed. Her dark hair fell to the floor and she placed it in the bin with the rags.

'Now give me your cap and coat, Hansl,' she said.

'What?'

'I am going to become Hansl. Are your identity papers in the pocket?'

'Yes, but –'

'Just do as she says, Hansl, and hurry.'

Hansl took off his overcoat and cap and handed them to Irena. 'What will I do if the police ask for my papers?' he moaned.

'When do the police ever stop schoolboys, Hansl?' Manfred snapped.

'But I'll be cold –'

'There are plenty of old clothes here to choose from,' Irena said, and handed him a brown leather jacket.

'It's horrible,' Hansl sniffed, close to tears.

'Not as horrible as what happened to its owner,' Irena said, slipping into Hansl's coat and cap. She was already wearing grey trousers like the ones Hansl wore to school.

Hansl stuck out his bottom lip and glared at Manfred. 'You promised I could be with you when you write on a bomb.'

Irena nodded. 'You shall. Follow me,' she said and led the way across to the loading shed. 'The crates nearest the loading door are the ones going off to Cambrai,' she said.

The wooden crates were not solid but simply a few planks nailed together to stop the bombs rolling off the lorry. 'Cambrai' was stamped in white letters on the nearest one. Irena pointed. 'Here. Reach between the planks and write whatever you like.'

Hansl cheered up and his eyes glittered. 'Can I help, Manfred?'

Manfred felt inside his trouser pocket and pulled out a piece of chalk. He passed it to his friend. 'There you go, Hansl.'

Hansl held the chalk as if it were a precious jewel. He spoke the words as he wrote: 'This one is for you, Tommy.'

'Now go,' Irena said.

'Go where?' Hansl asked.

'Back through the factory the way you came – and out Gate C,' she said as a crane creaked over their heads and began to lift the crate of bombs up and swing it towards the lorry.

Hansl turned. 'When will you be back?' he asked.

'Two days,' Manfred told him. 'We'll be in Cambrai tomorrow, I'll see Ernst and his Heinkel, then I'll come back on the empty lorry. I'll see to it your bomb goes on board Ernst's plane.'

'See you then,' Hansl said and ran off through the crates.

The last crate was loaded onto the lorry and the driver began to pull a sheet of green canvas over the top. 'Excuse me, sir,' Manfred said. 'We are riding with the bombs to Cambrai. My brother is a pilot there and he invited me and my friend Hansl. Can we climb in the back?'

The driver was a large, red-faced man with huge, hairy hands like a gorilla. 'You could, but you'd freeze. Come into the cab with me.'

'Thank you!' Manfred said and winked at Irena. He helped her into the cab and they settled down for the long journey to the airfield in conquered France.

They dozed most of the way. At a truck stop, the driver made sure they were fed, so Manfred didn't have to use his packets of food.

Irena stayed silent so her Polish accent didn't give her away. 'He's lost his voice,' Manfred lied.

Irena's head fell sideways and rested on the boy's shoulder. She was asleep again in moments. Manfred smiled and wrapped an arm around her thin shoulders before nodding off himself.

27

Cambrai Luftwaffe aerodrome, France
11 December 1940

It was noon the following day when they arrived at Cambrai aerodrome. The guards on the entrance were puzzled when they saw two children in the cab of a bomb lorry. They telephoned to the pilot quarters and Ernst arrived in a car. 'Yes, this is my brother,' he said cheerfully. 'But who is this?' he asked looking at Irena.

'It's my best friend, Hansl,' Manfred said and his eyes pleaded with his brother not to give him away.

'Of course!' the pilot laughed. 'Good to see you again . . . Hansl.' But on the trip across the airfield to Ernst's hut, he demanded, 'What's going on, Manfred? Who is this?'

As they walked from the car to the officer's room, Manfred explained. Ernst's face was pale with rage.

'So, you see, we have to save her,' Manfred finished.

'She is an under-human, Manfred. Her life is worthless. The Poles would not lift one finger to save you if you were in danger. But if the Gestapo ever found out about your idiot plan then your life really would be in danger. So would mine. Not to mention Mother, Father and Grandpa. That is the way the Gestapo thinks – if they find one rotten fish in the pond, they net the whole lot.'

Manfred sat quietly and waited for his brother's rage to die down. 'There is no risk, Ernst. You put her into your plane. You fly over to England. After you have dropped your last bomb, you let Irena jump out with a parachute.'

Ernst blew out his cheeks, 'You think this is a passenger service? An airline trip to the white cliffs of Dover? We can't just stick an extra passenger on board with no one noticing. What do I tell the crew? The gunners? The navigator? The engineer?'

'Do you never take passengers?' Manfred asked quietly.

'Never . . . well . . .'

'Yes?'

'We once took a spy. I dropped a man with a radio to report on the damage after the air raid on Biggin Hill.'

'Who sent the spy?'

'The Gestapo, of course.'

'And did the crew ask questions?'

'No, but the spy wasn't a dwarf – your under-human friend hardly looks like a Gestapo agent!'

Manfred stayed calm. 'No one ever asks questions when the Gestapo give an order. Next time you have a bombing raid, you load the bombs and tell the crew that an agent is joining them but they're not allowed to see him. The Gestapo insist.'

Ernst rubbed his eyes. 'Manfred, I have flown on

raids every night for the last week. Tonight I have a rest because there is fog over the east coast of England. But I am very tired. Too tired to argue.'

'So you will try my plan? Take Irena with you?'

The pilot looked at his brother. He looked at the frail and dark-eyed under-human. 'She has never jumped from a parachute before. The jump will probably kill her.'

'If I don't get to England, the Gestapo will *certainly* kill me,' the girl said quietly. 'What do I have to lose?' A parachute lay in the corner of Ernst's room. 'Show me what to do.'

Ernst Weiss spread his hands in defeat. 'Very well.'

28

Sheffield, England
11 December 1940

The policeman who came to the house after our blackout adventure was more scary than any villain Sherlock Holmes ever met. First, he told us that someone had reported we'd been sneaking around when we should have been in the shelter. We tried to explain we were Sherlock Holmes and Dr Watson on the trail of the Blackout Burglar, but he didn't seem to believe us. He said boys like me usually ended up going to something he called a reform school – a place like a prison for young criminals. He said the only reason he wasn't taking us to the police station was that he was a good friend of our dad. Our dad would be ashamed of us, he said, if he knew what we'd been up to.

'But he *does* know,' Sally argued. 'We telephoned him and asked him to tell us how he catches criminals.'

'The criminal needs motive, opportunity and knowledge,' I said, counting them off. 'And we need evidence. That's what we were doing out of the shelters. Gathering evidence!'

'You told me you were helping Warden Crane,' Mum said, and I could tell she was raging.

'We were,' I said. 'But –'

'And you told me you'd go straight to the nearest shelter when the siren went,' she said.

'We knew there wasn't going to be a raid!' I said. 'We telephoned Firbeck air base and they told us there was no raid!'

The policeman made a note. 'If Firbeck say they got a call, then you're off the hook . . . this time. But if I ever catch you out on the streets alone again, I'll lock you both away till it's time for you to collect your old-age pension.'

'And their dad will give them such a clip around the ear they'll be glad to get there,' Mum boiled. After she'd seen the policeman out, we were sent to bed with no supper, and no hot-water bottles, either.

The weeks after that were miserable. Mum didn't tell Dad, but she stopped us going out at all at night-time. I had to get straight home from school and wasn't even allowed to stop off at the shunting yards to do a bit of trainspotting with my mates. Sally had to peel potatoes and scrub the kitchen floor every night. When the siren sounded, we picked up our gas masks and followed Mum down to the public shelter like two lambs after their mother sheep. Someone once said 'War is hell'. For six weeks, I knew what they meant.

Then Dad came home on leave at the beginning of December. I ran home every night after school to play football in the back yard till it got too dark to see the heavy, brown ball – or until Mum got sick of hearing it bang against the wall and rattle off the dustbin. Sally wasn't happy because she was stuck in the kitchen with Mum, peeling potatoes and making the tea for when we came in.

'Girls don't play football,' Mum said and that was final.

Mind you, Sally liked having Dad in the house. Dad had stories about the pilots and the way they fought in the skies over the north. 'They are mad,' he said. 'They sit around on the grass, playing cards or writing letters or reading books. Then the alarm goes off and they drop everything, jump into their Hurricanes and Spitfires and they're off the ground in less than two minutes. They call it a "scramble", and it is. Some days they do that maybe five times.'

'Will we win?' Sally wanted to know.

'Probably,' Dad said. 'We shoot down more German bombers than they shoot down our fighters. In the end, they'll run out of bombs and bombers.'

Mum shook her head. 'They'll just keep making more,' she argued.

'Aha!' Dad said, wagging his finger. 'That's why our bombers have to fly over Germany and flatten their factories.'

'And they flatten ours. Though they haven't hit Sheffield yet,' Mum said and put her fingertips on the table. 'Touch wood.'

Dad supped his tea noisily. 'Of course, it's not just the planes that both sides lose – it's the pilots, too. We see a dozen planes take off, but we don't always see a dozen return. It's worst for the new pilots. Until they get a bit of experience, it's deadly. Train them all you like, but nothing prepares them for their first real battle. There was one lad arrived on Monday morning and he was scrambled before lunch. He never came back. When they went to his room, they found the poor lad hadn't even had time to unpack his case.'

'We'll run out of pilots before we run out of planes,' Mum sighed.

Dad shrugged. 'That's where we're a bit luckier than the Germans, I suppose. We have young men from all over the world – New Zealand, Canada, Australia. But the best pilots are the ones that escaped from Poland before the Nazis invaded. They don't speak much English, but by God they're brave – and they're good, too. All they want to do is get up there and shoot down Germans. As long as we have them at Firbeck, then Sheffield should be safe.'

'It's a bomber's moon this week,' I said.

'It is, son. Your mum and me used to like the moonlight. We went out for walks over Attercliffe Common, didn't we, Betty?'

Mum seemed to be blushing and made herself busy gathering plates to wash up. 'That was a long time ago,' she muttered as she disappeared into the kitchen.

Dad leaned forward so I could smell the Brylcreem in his hair. 'I quite fancy walking your mum down to the Tivoli tonight and seeing a film. She needs a break.'

'Good idea, Dad,' Sally said.

'Will you two be all right on your own for the evening?' he asked.

'Oh, yes!' Sally cried and her eyes sparkled. 'We were always all right playing out until –'

She stopped. Mum hadn't told Dad about the Blackout Burglar or me and Sally being suspects.

'Until what?'

'Erm . . . well . . . ' Sally stammered.

'We were always all right playing out until . . . it got too dark,' I said. 'But you take Mum to the pictures and we'll be fine, won't we, Sal?'

'Fine,' she agreed.

'Thanks, kids,' Dad said. 'I'll give you a shilling each. You can spend it at the sweet shop, maybe? Get some wine gums and eat them while you listen to the radio. *Sexton Blake*'s on tonight, isn't he?'

'Thanks, Dad,' I grinned. Sally caught my eye. We both knew we wouldn't be listening to any radio. There was a burglar to catch and Sherlock and the real Sexton would be cracking the crime.

Dad went into the kitchen to tell Mum about his plan. She argued that it was wrong to leave us in the house alone.

'It's my last night,' Dad said firmly. 'I get the bus back to Firbeck tomorrow evening. I won't take no for an answer.'

And so it was settled. Mum took so long getting ready, I thought Dad was going to wear out the carpet with all his marching up and down. 'We'll miss the main film never mind the B movie if you don't hurry up!' he shouted up the stairs.

'I'm just putting on a bit of that perfume you got me last Christmas.'

'Will you be ready before *this* Christmas?' Dad cried. Then he came back into the living room and sat down to wait. 'So what happened in your Blackout Burglar story?' he asked us. 'Did he get caught?'

I took a deep breath so I could get my thoughts together before I explained – I didn't want to mention that we'd become the chief suspects.

'We have four main suspects. The trouble is, our detectives haven't any evidence. We're a bit stuck.'

'We had the same thing at Firbeck camp. When the pilots went on a mission, someone was going through their lockers and taking small amounts of cash – just a half-crown here and there so the pilots hardly missed it, or didn't want to make a fuss about it.'

'Same as the Blackout Burglar,' Sally said.

'There was a smudge of oil on one of the lockers that was robbed, so we thought it could be one of the mechanics that look after the planes. The trouble is there are twenty of them on the base. Nineteen were innocent but they were all suspects.'

'It's awful being a suspect when you know you're not to blame,' I muttered bitterly.

'So what did you do, Dad?'

'Set a trap. We got one of the pilots to carry a bag of money into the workshops and complain that his wife had sent him the winnings from his football pools coupon. She had cashed the cheque and brought the money to the base. He'd only have to put it in the bank tomorrow. I said I'd put it in his locker and he said it was locker 24, but he had no idea how much was in the bag.'

'And the thief fell for it?'

'Oh, yes. The pilots were scrambled that afternoon and as soon as they took off I was hiding in the locker room, watching. The mouse nibbled at the cheese within ten minutes, and I nabbed him.'

'Did you hang him, Dad?' Sally asked.

Dad laughed. 'No. We didn't even give him a trial. I mean, he could have said he wasn't to blame for the twenty other little thefts. We just made sure the officer in charge of the workshops gave him every filthy, smelly, heavy and dangerous job he could – emptying hot oil from the engines, sweeping up when the rest of the mechanics had finished work, weeding the flowerbeds outside the huts, unloading the food lorries. There's more than one way to punish a thief!'

At quarter to seven, Mum came downstairs, looking like one of those dummies you see in clothes-shop windows and wearing a hat with more feathers than a pigeon. As it was so late, they rushed out of the door with a quick, 'Goodbye, be good,' finally leaving us on our own.

Sally and I sat back. She reached inside her gas mask and pulled out our list of suspects. 'One of these is phoning the Home Guard and getting the air-raid siren started,' she said. 'All we have to do is follow them.'

'How do two of us follow four people, Sherlock?' I asked.

'Good question.'

'Do you have a good answer?'

'Mmmm. That's the sort of thing Dr Watson can work out.'

'Thanks, Sal.'

And after five minutes, while we found our hats and coats, scarves and torches, I had an idea. 'We set a trap, like Dad said. We tell them we know someone who is really careless with their money and leaves their house open. Then we watch the house like a mousetrap.'

Sally shook her head slowly. 'If I was the burglar, I'd set a false air-raid warning off.'

'I agree.'

'But they won't have time to do that tonight.'

'They'll do it tomorrow night,' I said.

'And we'll be stuck in the house with Mum again tomorrow night,' she said. 'If the air-raid siren *does* go, she'll drag us off to the shelter. We can't watch our mousetrap.'

'We need to tell her we're going to a different shelter – that's it! There's a church youth club on a Thursday night. We tell her we're going there. If there's a siren, we'll go to the cellars of the church hall the way they do.'

'So we pick a house – let's make it Mrs Grimley's. We tell our suspects she's had a win on the football pools and she's stuffed the money in that teapot of hers.'

'We can't tell all our suspects tonight,' Sally said.

I agreed. 'I think Mr Cutter the teacher and Mrs Haddock at the sweet shop are into the black market,' I said. 'But Vicar Treadwell and Sergeant Proctor from the Home Guard are the ones that shouldn't be wandering round the streets in the blackout.'

'I'll go to the vicarage and tell the vicar about Mrs Grimley's winnings,' Sally offered. 'I always wanted to have a look at the graveyard at night. See if there are any ghosts around.'

I never understood Sally.

'I've got to track down Sergeant Proctor, then. If I find Warden Crane, maybe he'll be able to tell me where Mr Proctor hangs out.'

We stepped out into the street and looked up at the sky. Flurries of sleet blew in our faces as clouds raced across the moon. 'There'll be no raid tonight anyway,' I said. 'Make sure you're back here before ten o'clock. We don't want Mum to know we've been out. Best of luck, Sherlock,' I said.

'Best of luck, Watson,' Sally replied.

29

It wasn't hard to find Mr Crane. 'Put out the light!' he was crying in the damp streets.

He caught sight of me on the corner of Attercliffe Road. 'Why, if it isn't young Billy Thomas. Haven't seen you for a few weeks. I thought you and young Sally were my runners?'

'Mum kept us in for bunking off school,' I lied.

'Can't say I blame you,' he chuckled. 'I made a good living on the stage as an actor, you know. School never taught me that. School just taught me to pass my exams so I could get a good job in the steelworks.'

'I want to be a policeman when I leave school,' I said. 'I don't know what good learning about William the Conqueror's going to do me.'

We walked along, huddled against the flurries of sleet. 'Time for a tea break,' the warden said, before I could ask him about Sergeant Proctor.

'Are you going to the wardens' post next to the Stanhope Street shelter?' I asked.

'Ah, no, that's a boring place, my boy. It's full of wardens! I have struck up a friendship with a generous lady in the area. She expects me to drop by for a cup of tea most evenings around eight, unless there's an air-raid warning, of course. I'm sure there'll be enough in the pot for you,' he said.

So I found myself turning into the back yard of

Mrs Grimley's house. Music was playing on the radio and Warden Crane had to knock twice to be heard. At last the door was opened by a young man in a pilot's uniform – Paul Grimley.

'Hello, Warden! Mum's just been telling me she expected you around this time. And you've brought your young runner with you, too? Billy Thomas, isn't it? There's plenty of tea in the pot. I got a pound of the stuff from one of the spivs that sells it at Firbeck.'

Warden Crane brushed the damp off his coat as he led the way into the warm living room. 'Black-market tea, Mrs Grimley!' he cried. 'Better be careful – young Billy here is planning to be a copper when he grows up. He might report you – get in a bit of practice!'

The Grimleys laughed and set a place at the table with a scone Mrs Grimley had baked for Paul's visit.

'I finished my training yesterday so I start flying missions tomorrow. We get twenty-four hours' leave before we start flying into real action,' he explained.

'We've had nothing but false alarms round here,' his mother complained. 'My shoes have worn a path from here to the shelter the times I've been there and back. I'm thinking of staying in the house next time.'

'Don't!' her son said. The pilot put down his cup and leaned forward so we could hear him speaking in a low voice. 'Everything could change this week,' he said.

'We're going to be bombed?' Mrs Grimley squawked.

'Hush, Mother. Careless talk costs lives. I shouldn't say anything, but there's a rumour going around the base that there'll be a raid on a northern town while there's a bomber's moon – over the next few days.

'Hull, Manchester, Leeds or Sheffield. We're not sure. But Mr Churchill has spies in Germany that tell us it'll be this week.'

'Ohhhh!' Mrs Grimley said. 'What if they hit this house? When your dad died, I cashed his insurance. Over a thousand pounds. That'll go up in smoke if the house gets hit. I was saving it for you, Paul. After the war, you can buy a house of your own with that sort of money.'

'Put it in the bank, Mother.'

'Oh, we've had that discussion,' Warden Crane said. 'Mrs Grimley reckons banks get robbed – she's seen it in the cinema.'

'Houses get robbed, too,' I reminded her.

She shook her head crossly. 'Nobody'll find it under me mattress,' she said. 'Nobody knows it's there and I'm not telling anyone.'

'A German incendiary bomb would find it,' Paul told her.

'I'll go to the bank tomorrow,' the woman sighed.

'I'll give you a reference,' Warden Crane said.

'A what?'

'The banks won't take money from just anyone – I mean, you could be a spiv trying to stash away your illegal earnings,' Paul explained.

'I'm not! If anyone in the bank says I'm a spiv, I'll . . . I'll crack them with me umbrella!' Mrs Grimley snapped. 'I sell the odd ration of sugar to somebody what needs it, but I'm not a crook.'

'No, Ma,' Paul said quietly. 'Go to the bank tomorrow and open an account. Mr Crane here will write a letter to say you're a respectable citizen –'

'I'll drop the letter off in the morning,' the warden promised. 'You can start paying in your money on Friday morning.'

Mrs Grimley nodded in resignation.

'You'll just have to take a chance and hope the house isn't hit by a bomb tomorrow night,' Warden Crane added. 'The money will be safe after that. I've been telling you for weeks, haven't I, Billy?'

'Yes, Mr Crane,' I agreed.

Now I knew where Mrs Grimley kept her money, I could use it to bait the trap. I'd find Sergeant Proctor of the Home Guard tonight and drop the word to Mr Cutter in class tomorrow. Sally would be telling the vicar tonight and we'd call in to Mrs Haddock's sweet shop and gossip about the Grimley money while we were there. The Blackout Burglar would arrange a false alarm for tomorrow night, go for Mrs Grimley's money, and we'd be waiting.

Perfect. Sherlock Holmes never laid such a perfect trap in his life.

181

I really enjoyed my tea and scone and couldn't keep the smile off my face.

Perfect. Nothing could go wrong.

Cambrai Luftwaffe aerodrome, France
11 December 1940

Ernst made up a bed for Irena and his brother on the floor of his room. Manfred was amazed at the food the pilot brought them.

'Yes, we are the knights of the air and Herr Hitler makes sure we eat well. Fresh vegetables, good cuts of meat, well cooked. We even have sugar for our coffee and real eggs for breakfast.'

Irena ate like a sparrow. Her stomach was so shrunken by starvation she struggled to swallow the tender steak in rich gravy. Even Ernst's heart began to soften. 'In England – when you land – they will put you in a camp like Dachau,' he said gently.

Irena nodded. 'But at least they will treat me like a friend – a Pole – not an enemy and an under-human.'

'We'll put you in the bomb bay with some blankets,' Ernst said. 'It will be a cold and noisy couple of hours.'

'Just like the factory,' Irena said and gave a faint smile. 'I am used to it.'

'When the last bomb has gone, you will count to ten then jump – no point in you jumping into the fire that last bomb makes!'

'Are you bombing London?' Manfred asked.

'We don't know yet. They'll tell us tomorrow afternoon before we set out. If everyone knew about tomorrow's targets today then an English spy could pass on a message. They would be waiting with their Spitfires and Hurricanes. All I know is the moon is nearly full and the weather forecast says there will be a clear sky, so we are sure to attack somewhere in England. Now, make yourself comfortable.'

'Can I have a look around your bomber before I leave?' Manfred asked.

'Of course. We'll ride across on the bomb loader tomorrow night and I'll show you the controls while we load. Irena can slip into the bomb bay and you can jump out before takeoff. Ride back in the empty bomb loader and we'll make sure the truck back to Dachau is waiting for you.'

Manfred lay back on the blanket bed and smiled. It was all going to plan. Irena would escape and he would have had an exciting few days away from Herr Gruber and school. Perfect, he mumbled as he dropped off to sleep. Just perfect.

30

Sheffield, England
12 December 1940

Mum helped us on with our coats. 'These are damp. I thought you stayed in last night?' she said, suspicious as a policeman's wife.

'We went to the sweet shop to spend the shillings Dad gave us,' Sally said quickly. She said it quicker than I could think it. Sometimes she really made me feel like dim Dr Watson to her Sherlock.

'What did you buy?' Mum asked.

'Gobstoppers,' I said, at the same time as Sally said, 'Liquorice allsorts.'

'I had liquorice allsorts,' Sally explained, 'because they're made in Sheffield and Miss Goodwin at our school says we shouldn't waste petrol moving sweets around the country when there's a war on. *Save fuel for battle*, the poster says. Billy had gobstoppers because he has a big gob that needs stopping.'

'Did you save me any liquorice allsorts?' Mum asked.

'No, sorry, Mum. Billy finished his gobstoppers then ate the last of the liquorice allsorts.'

'I never!' I cried. And that was the truth. We hadn't even *been* to the sweet shop, we'd been too busy.

'You're a greedy lad, Billy,' Mum said.

I chewed my lip and glared at Sally. She smiled sweetly.

'Mum's right, Billy,' she said.

'I'll see you tonight,' Dad called from the living room. 'I'm catching the seven o'clock tram back to Firbeck.'

'Will we have time for a kickabout in the back lane after school?' I asked.

'We can kick a ball in the front street if you like. It's safe enough. Not many people have the petrol for cars,' he said.

'But lots of people have windows,' Mum said. 'Now get off to school, and no hanging about on the way back.'

Sally and I hurried down the street. There were puddles on the cracked pavement and in the tram tracks, but the sky was clearing and the cold wind was pushing at the silver-grey barrage balloons. Trams rattled by making as much noise as the steelworks. It would be a bomber's moon tonight with no cloud to save some poor northern town, if Paul Grimley's spy report was right.

'I told the vicar about Mrs Grimley having her savings in the larder, in the meat safe at the back,' she said. 'He said he'd call round and have a word next Monday.'

'Her savings are under her mattress,' I said.

'How do you know that?'

185

'She told her Paul last night.'

'Eeeeh!' Sally cried and pointed at a faded poster warning about careless talk. 'She wants to read that.'

'It doesn't matter where the money really is – we just want to see if the vicar goes into the house now he knows there's money there. Let's tell Mrs Haddock. Have you still got the shilling Dad gave you?'

'Yes, but we might as well spend *yours*. We need to get you out of that bad habit of being greedy,' Sally laughed, and ran off before I could kick her skinny backside.

My sister was already in the dusty shop chatting when I got there. 'And have you had any more trouble with the burglar trying to break into your safe?' she was asking.

'No, I haven't, child. But I keep the key in me knickers so any burglar would have a job to get in.'

'Eeeeh, our Billy was round at Mrs Grimley's house last night and she has *thousands* of pounds in the house and she doesn't have a safe or a key in her knickers,' Sally said.

'Always was a stupid woman, Ada Grimley,' Mrs Haddock said and folded her arms as if she were disgusted. 'Went to school with her, you know.'

'She's got the insurance money from her husband dying,' Sally went on. 'She keeps it under her mattress.'

'He's a lucky feller, her husband,' Mrs Haddock said, with a smirk.

'Lucky being married to Mrs Grimley?'

'No. Lucky to be dead. Sharing a spot in the churchyard has *got* to be better than sharing a house with a miserable trout like her. I never liked the woman. Never.'

'Her Paul's getting her to put the money in the bank on Friday,' I put in. 'I guess the Blackout Burglar needs to get there tonight.'

Mrs Haddock turned her little eyes on me. 'There's some people say you know more about this burglar than most.'

'It's not true!' I shouted.

'Off you go,' she said, reaching into a cupboard for her coat and hat. 'I need to shut the shop.'

'You've only just opened,' Sally pointed out.

'Yes. And now I'm just closing,' she said, bustling us through the door. 'I have to see a man about a job that needs doing.' And she locked the door behind her.

'I bet you do,' I said, as she shuffled down the street. 'She's off to see her burglar. I think we may have solved the case before she steps into the trap. Mrs Haddock gets the gossip in her sweet shop and passes it onto her burglar.'

'Her mate, your teacher, Mr Cutter?'

'Dunno. She isn't headed towards the school. Maybe she has someone else that does the breaking-in. She doesn't look the sort to go climbing through windows.'

'No,' Sally agreed. 'The key in her knickers would rattle against the window frame.'

I had to laugh. I left Sally to go in the girls' entrance to school and walked along to the boys' yard. Lads were playing marbles, skimming cigarette cards or smashing into one another playing British Bulldog, while others chased around playing Nazis and Brits.

Mr Cutter was on yard duty, wrapping his hands round a warm mug of tea and waiting to blow the whistle. It looked as if he wanted to get in out of the cold, but even the cold was better than teaching us, so he supped slowly at the tea.

'Can I have a quick word, Mr Cutter?' I asked.

'What is it, Thomas?'

'I'm a bit worried about an old lady that lives in the next street to me and I need to tell someone – someone who can be trusted – so I thought of you.'

His thin mouth turned down in the odd way he had of smiling. 'Ask away, lad, I am a pillar of the community. It's my job to help everyone, young or old.'

So I told him the same story we'd told Mrs Haddock. I thought his breathing was getting faster as his breath steamed in the cold morning air.

'I'll . . . erm . . . I'll inform the proper authorities,' he said stiffly. 'I'll do it now. I'll use the headmaster's telephone while you're in assembly.'

'Thank you, sir. I knew I was right to trust you.'

'Of course, Thomas,' he said. He checked his watch and placed the whistle to his mouth. 'Oh, and Thomas, do *not* tell anyone else. Let's keep this between ourselves, shall we?'

'Careless talk costs money, eh, sir?' I said.

'Exactly, Thomas. I couldn't have put it better myself.' He took a deep breath and gave a blast on the whistle so loud it nearly deafened me.

All day, Mr Cutter kept catching my eye as if we shared a secret. I'd never seen him smile so much. I'll swear he smiled three times that Thursday when usually he smiled about three times a year.

31

Firbeck air base, England
12 December 1940

Paul Grimley had felt edgy all day. For weeks now
the pilots had heard the reports on the air battles in
the South. The Luftwaffe had only attacked the North
once – a raid on Sunderland. The Germans had flown
too far from home for the Messerschmitt fighters
to come along and protect them – the planes didn't
carry enough fuel. So the RAF in the North shot the
bombers down like ducks on a fairground rifle range.
The pilots from Firbeck flew up to join in the battle,
but they arrived too late.

'The war will be over before we see a German,'
Lieutenant Bronisław Maniak moaned to Paul that
morning. The Polish airman had flown fighters in the
short and hopeless defence of Poland. He'd escaped
just as the Germans reached his airfield and gone
straight into the RAF.

'No,' his friend Paul said. 'They'll have to start
attacking the factories up here soon. They can't win
the war in the air because as fast as they shoot down a
Spitfire, we build a new one.'

Bronisław waved his fingers like a magician.
'You're a real Alexander, aren't you?'

'Who?'

'That mind-reader – Alexander the Crystal Seer,' he teased. 'You can see into the minds of Hermann Göring and his Luftwaffe. So, Alexander, what town are they going to bomb up here?'

Paul took the question seriously. 'It has to be Sheffield, doesn't it? The greatest steel city in the world. They have to stop us making the crankshafts for the Spitfires, and we have the only factory in Britain that makes them.'

Bronisław nodded. 'Thank you, Alexander, The Man Who Knows . . . now can you tell me *when* they're going to attack? If you can tell me which day the Germans are coming, I can go off on holiday and come back here in time to welcome them.'

Paul wandered over to the window of the hut and looked up at the cold, clear sky. 'It's a bomber's moon. Why not tonight?'

Bronisław threw his head back and laughed. 'There goes my holiday. I'd better hang around to shoot Jerry down, I suppose.'

Paul walked to the door. 'See you later.'

'Where are you off to?'

'To practise,' Paul said. 'I'm going on the firing range, then I'm taking up the Hurricane to fly over Sheffield and get a feel for the place in daylight, in case we have to fight there tonight.'

'I'm coming with you, Alexander the Crystal Seer!' Bronisław Maniak cried. 'I'll fight you.'

Paul nodded. 'Good idea. We'll shoot at one another with the movie cameras and see who comes out on top. It'll sharpen us up for the real thing.'

They jogged across the grass to the hangars where their Hurricanes sat.

The young guard said, 'Halt, who goes there?'

Paul peered at him. 'You're new. Where's Eric Thomas – Tommy – the usual guard?'

'Home on leave in Sheffield, sir.'

'You should have seen that, Alexander,' Bronisław Maniak joked.

'Ah, well, here are our identity papers,' Paul said, passing them over. 'We're off on a training exercise.'

'Best of luck, gentlemen,' the guard said and saluted.

The Hurricanes' cameras were loaded with film and their tanks with fuel. They roared off into the sky and headed west. Below them, the barrage balloons hung like dead elephants and the factories belched smoke in shades from white to charcoal. The River Don was a dull, leaden colour; the roofs and the winter grass in the parks and commons were frosted silver. Sheffield was a black-and-white photograph below them.

Bronisław waggled his wings as a sign for the dogfight to begin. Paul was ready for it. He hauled back on the joystick so his Hurricane climbed so steeply it seemed to be standing on its tail. Then it rolled over into a loop and fell like an arrow onto Bronisław

Maniak's tail . . . except he wasn't there! Paul jerked his head around to see where the other Hurricane was and saw it, just too late, right behind him.

Bronisław was pressing the firing button on his camera as Paul Grimley rolled away. The Pole followed and pulled alongside, laughing. He placed his mask over his mouth and spoke into the microphone: 'You'll have to do better than that, comrade. You're flying a Hurricane now, not a Wellington bomber.'

Paul pulled ahead and as Bronisław accelerated, he pulled the wing flaps to slow himself. Bronisław Maniak shot past and Paul found himself on his friend's tail again. The sights on his windscreen were filled with the Pole's Hurricane and he fired the camera gun.

A mile below, boys on their way to school looked up open-mouthed.

'It's a Messerschmitt against a Spitfire – I bet the Spitfire wins!' Eddie Duncan cried.

His mates jeered. 'Even my auntie Gladys knows a couple of Hurricanes when she sees them,' one of the lads said, as the planes flew low over the tops of the barrage balloons and disappeared to the east.

The film of Paul Grimley's practice fight had been developed by the afternoon and the squadron sat and watched it in the blacked-out room that served as their cinema.

'Fly straight level for more than twenty seconds and you're dead,' the squadron leader said. 'That's the rule.'

'Why is that, sir?'

'Why? Because you'll have a German fighter on your tail.'

'But they won't send fighters this far north, will they, sir?'

The officer sighed. 'Good habits, Grimley. You have to learn good habits if you want to survive. And look at what happened when you shot at Maniak –'

The film projector rolled and showed a Hurricane in the centre of the frame. 'Dead centre,' Paul boasted.

'Dead pilot – you,' his leader said. 'That shot took ten seconds – *ten*! In ten seconds, two things could have happened. First, your enemy's pals would have you in their sights and you'd be a goner. Second, your own guns would overheat and jam. The best pilots fire for four seconds and no more.' The man shook his head. 'Let's hope we have another few weeks of training before we have to send you up against a real enemy raid.'

'Grimley says they're coming tonight,' Bronisław Maniak interrupted. 'It's a bomber's moon and Alexander the Crystal Seer says it's Sheffield's turn.'

'In that case we're all ready . . . except Grimley. Let's hope he doesn't shoot one of us down by mistake.'

The men laughed and went back to card games,

reading books, darts practice or writing letters home. But now there was a feeling of tension, as if they believed Paul Grimley's mystic power.

When they went to check that their planes were armed and ready – as they did every evening after training flights – the pilots were extra-careful to check that their ammunition drums were moving freely, that the mechanics had the engines running sweetly, and that the controls were greased and working.

One or two even went back after supper to write letters that began, *'If you are reading this, it means I have been killed. . .'*

32

Sheffield, England
12 December 1940

I waited for Sally after school and we talked through the last details of our plan. We wouldn't try to stop the Blackout Burglar, but we'd follow him or her and see where they put the loot. Then we'd go to the wardens' post and telephone the police.

'Should we go into Mrs Grimley's house first? Mark the notes with invisible ink?' Sally asked.

'We haven't got any invisible ink,' I said.

'Lemon juice. Miss Goodwin showed us how the spies do it in France.'

I blew out my cheeks. 'You have more interesting lessons than us. We just get told about the crusades, and I've got ten dates to learn for a test tomorrow. Bo-ring!'

'So, shall we buy a lemon?'

'No. The burglar will probably be watching Mrs Grimley's door to see when she leaves. He'd see us go in and that would ruin it. No, we'll stick to the plan.'

We set off at a run so we could get home and have as much time as we could with Dad before he went back to Firbeck.

Mum had cooked a special tea of mincemeat and dumplings.

'This'll put hairs on your chest,' said Dad, tucking in. 'I wish we got fed like this at Firbeck. I'll swear the cow we had in the Sunday stew died before the war.'

At half-past six, we said goodbye, then he went off to catch the tram.

'Mum,' Sally said. 'Is it all right if me and Billy go to the church youth club? It starts in half an hour.'

'Youth club? I thought you didn't like that Vicar Treadwell!'

'Yes, but some of my friends want to go to play table tennis.'

'I'll go along to keep an eye on her,' I offered.

Mum smiled. 'That's nice. A lad that looks after his little sister. You'll keep her out of trouble, I'm sure.'

As soon as Mum and Dad had left the house, Sally and I armed ourselves with torches and put on extra socks in case it was cold standing around waiting for the mousetrap to snap shut. We were so close to catching the Blackout Burglar now.

Cambrai Luftwaffe aerodrome, France
12 December 1940

Ernst Weiss returned to the hut as darkness was falling. Irena and Manfred had rolled up their blanket beds and tidied them away in the cupboard. They had made sandwiches from the mounds of bread and bacon left

197

over after breakfast and lunch. Manfred wore his school coat and cap, but Irena was hidden under a greatcoat and felt hat. She carried an empty cardboard suitcase so she looked to the aircraft crew like a spy with a radio. A very small spy, but no one ever asked questions about the Gestapo and its plans.

'Ready?' Ernst asked.

'So? Where will Irena be going?' Manfred asked.

The pilot turned to a map on the wall and jabbed a finger at the north of England. 'A new target tonight – a place called Sheffield.'

'I've never heard of it,' Manfred said.

'The Steel City,' Irena said quietly. 'We learned about it in our geography lessons back in Poland.'

'The Steel City,' Ernst agreed. 'We'll aim for the east of the city where all the steelworks are. It's a good place to drop you, Irena. Once we've bombed the factories, you're pretty sure to land in the countryside – Attercliffe Common or the fields to the east. After that it's up to you to make your way into the town and tell your story.'

'Thank you,' Irena said quietly.

Ernst looked stern. 'If anyone ever found out what I had done to help an enemy of the Nazis escape, they would kill me, probably very slowly. And they would be sure to find out how Manfred helped, so he would have to die, too. You see what that means?'

'When I tell my story to the English, I'll tell them

I had no help. I hid myself on a bomber and stole a parachute from one of the crew,' Irena said.

'You have never met Manfred and Ernst Weiss.'

Irena's eyes opened in wonder. 'I have never even heard of anyone called Manfred and Ernst Weiss!' she cried.

Ernst laughed. 'You'll do – you know, I almost hope you make it!'

'Me, too,' Irena said.

Manfred checked his watch. 'Time to go.'

He led the way across the square of concrete to where the crew wagons stood. A hundred young men were crowding onto the waiting wagons. If anyone saw the tiny figure in a hat carrying a suitcase and the boy in a school cap, they said nothing. They rode in silence across the airfield to the planes, where winches were hauling up bomb loads into their bellies. Each crew member remembered friends who had made this short journey and never returned. Each crew member wondered if this would be his last time. Some men smoked a final cigarette and some supped at small flasks of brandy.

The wagon stopped and the men climbed down. They walked over the frosty grass by the edge of the runway to their Heinkels, Junkers and Dorniers. The first wave of pathfinders were already roaring past them with chattering propellers blasting their faces with hot and oily engine smoke.

As Manfred approached his brother's Heinkel, he saw the last rack of five bombs being lifted steadily on a winch. In the dim light, he saw there were words chalked on the side of a bomb: 'This one is for you, Tommy.' And suddenly he felt the ache of missing Hansl and being hundreds of miles from home.

Ernst led them up a ladder into the crew section at the front and quickly directed Irena back to the bomb bay. The bomb-aimer was closing the doors and looked up in surprise.

'Remember Biggin Hill?' the pilot said.

'Yes, sir.'

'This is another gentleman from the Gestapo. We are taking him for a ride to Sheffield. Make sure he gets away safely after the last bomb has gone. Apart from that, forget you have seen him and don't try to speak to him.'

'Haven't seen him, sir.'

'Give him a parachute and a blanket to keep him warm.'

'Yes, sir.'

'Good luck,' Ernst said.

Irena stayed silent.

Manfred was waiting in the cockpit, wide-eyed and full of joy at being on a warplane. Ernst returned to explain the controls.

'This is the magneto to start the motors,' he said. 'I'll start them up so you get a feel of the noise we have to put up with for hours, and then you can climb back down.'

The engine on the right whirred and popped and exploded into life, followed by the one on the left, until the whole aeroplane was shaking. The engineer reported on all the checks he needed to do, the pressures and the performance. 'All fine!' he shouted at last, and Ernst eased back on the throttle till the warm engines were purring.

'Time to go,' the pilot said. 'See you before Christmas, I hope.'

'Thanks, Ernst – I'll never forget this trip.'

The brothers hugged and slapped one another on the back.

But as Manfred headed for the door, he heard the loud blast of a car horn and the screech of tyres on the tarmac. He stepped back into the cabin and looked out. A large, grey Mercedes had pulled up in front of the nose of Ernst's Heinkel, blocking its way.

Ernst threw open a side window to call angrily, 'What are you playing at, you buffoon?'

A tall man in a black leather coat had stepped from the car and was looking up at the cabin. Manfred stayed in the shadows behind his brother and watched. He felt sickness rising in his throat. He knew the man and he knew he'd already received the only warning he would ever get.

This time Manfred knew he would be shot.

33

'I am Gauführer Linz – Gestapo chief in the Munich region,' the Nazi officer shouted up to the Heinkel's cabin.

'I don't care if you're Hitler's pet dog. Get out of my way.'

'You cannot speak to a Gestapo officer like that.'

'You are not in Munich now – you have no power in this airfield. Get out of my way.'

The Gestapo chief stood firm. 'I am following the trail of an escaped Polish prisoner – a girl called Irena Karski. A kapo in Dachau munitions factory thinks he saw her climbing into the cab of a bomb delivery truck.'

'What has that got to do with me?' Ernst cried.

'The prisoner was in the company of a known traitor – Manfred Weiss, your brother. Have you seen him?'

'Yes – he stayed here last night. I saw him onto an empty truck heading back home just ten minutes ago,' the pilot lied.

'And was the girl with him?'

'A girl? Have you come all this way to arrest a girl?'

Gauführer Linz jabbed a furious finger at the cockpit. 'We cannot let the under-humans escape. We have to find her, take her back and execute her in front of all the Dachau slaves.'

'Wish I could help, Gauführer Linz, but she

probably jumped on a train at Cambrai and she'll be at the English Channel by now. You'd be best searching the ports.'

'Do not tell me where I should be searching,' the Gestapo officer raged.

'Give my love to my brother when you find him,' Ernst said, then shouted to the crew below the cockpit, 'Ladders away – chocks away – as soon as that car is shifted, we'll get on with the raid.'

Gauführer Linz stalked back to the car, pointed in the direction of the main gate and drove off. Manfred felt the engine note rise and the plane move forward. 'Ernst! I'm still on board.'

'I know – let's talk about it later. Sit in that seat by the navigator, put on your seatbelt and let me get this thing on course for England.'

Manfred obeyed and sat down trembling. He wasn't sure if it was the plane or the shock that was making him shudder till his teeth rattled. As the plane left the ground, his stomach seemed to jump into his mouth, and the roar of the engines as it climbed left him half deaf. At last, the plane reached its ceiling and Ernst handed the controls to his co-pilot. He stepped back to sit next to Manfred.

'If you'd got out back in Cambrai, your friend Gauführer Linz would have snatched you in no time. Our mother would have killed me. So let's keep you out of his way for tonight. When we land, we'll think

203

of what to do. Maybe you can stay with me at the air base till the heat is off.'

'Thanks, Ernst – sorry I've got you into so much trouble.'

'Ha! You're not so much trouble as Spitfires over England,' said the pilot. 'Well, not quite. But there's no reason why Gauführer Linz should think we helped his slave escape. It's such a crazy plan, he'll never believe we could do it. So forget about him and enjoy the flight.' He patted his brother on the shoulder.

As they sped up the east coast of England, Ernst pointed out the places they were passing below. The other Heinkels and Junkers kept them company and made Manfred feel safe. The mass of German planes looked too solid for a few British fighter planes to damage. Beneath them, the dark land stood out like a black cutout set against the glittering moon-blue sea.

'Turn west-north-west,' the navigator said into his microphone. Target three-hundred and eighty kilometres.'

'The first wave should be there by now,' Ernst said. 'We'll be about two hours to target. Bomb fuses primed?'

'Primed and ready.'

Ernst took off his microphone mask and spoke to Manfred. 'Why don't you go into the bomb bay? You can see your bomb drop and say goodbye to your Polish friend.'

Manfred nodded and squeezed through the narrow cabin door into the main fuselage. It was lit with a faint green light that made the bomb-aimer look like a dummy on a ghost train ride.

Irena sat in a corner, face shadowed by the hat, holding a blanket tightly around her. She looked up, puzzled, as Manfred climbed over the sections of airframe and sat down beside her. 'Not long now.'

'Why are you here?' she asked.

'Came along for the ride,' he told her.

The young airman in the bomb bay sent a message to Ernst Weiss to say the bombs had been slid into place and were ready to drop as soon as they reached the target.

'I hope they hit factories not houses,' Irena cried. 'I don't want innocent people to die.'

'They won't – only if their name is Tommy,' Manfred laughed.

The engines were loud. But the sound of bullets exploding into the Heinkel was louder and the whole plane lurched. Manfred was thrown towards the open bomb doors and Irena snatched at his coat and tugged him back.

'What was that?' Manfred called to the airman.

The airman listened in his headphones. 'We're under attack. Spitfires from the English Channel defences – Group 11. They've done no harm.'

'Will we crash?'

'No, but we'll face a lot worse than that when we get over the target. They may send up some fighters from Fighter Command Group 12 in the Midlands, too. Then we're into Group 13 in the North. The sooner we drop these bombs, the happier I'll be. We could be in for a rough ride home!'

The Heinkel turned north and kept the English coast under the port wing.

34

Firbeck air base, England
12 December 1940

The control centre at Firbeck was underground, safe from bombs that could fall if the Luftwaffe decided to attack the airfield.

An RAF officer wore a uniform bright with medals and brass buttons and gold braid. 'Have we tracked the German's X-Gerat beam?'

'Yes, sir.'

'What's tonight's target?'

'Sheffield, sir.'

The officer looked closely at the map. 'If they get close to the steelworks, they could cause a lot of damage.'

'Yes, sir.'

The officer took a deep breath. 'And we can bend this X-Gerat beam, you say? Send them off course?'

'We can bend it about five degrees, sir.'

'Do it.'

The man at the flickering green screen turned a knob and heard the machine hum. He paused. His hand hung waiting over a dial. 'Five degrees, sir – that takes the bombers directly over the city centre. To be exact, the Duke of Wellington pub in Carlisle Street.'

'Yes.'

'There could be a lot of people round there, sir.'

'That's why they have shelters,' the officer said sharply. 'I have to make a choice – lose the factories and lose the war, or risk the lives of a few people.'

'Yes, sir.'

For half a minute there was no sound but the humming of the machines. At last, the officer said quietly, 'Bend the beam. Let them bomb the city centre. And, Parkinson?'

'Yes, sir?'

'You do not repeat what happened here in this bunker tonight.'

Pause.

'No, sir.'

The call to the pilots came five minutes later, at 18:47 hours. Bronisław Maniak took the call and repeated it out loud as he heard the orders.

'Enemy bombers spotted on radar off the east coast . . . three flights of about a hundred each . . . turning west at Hull . . . probable target Sheffield, South Yorkshire or West Yorkshire . . . scramble Group 13 . . . seek and destroy . . . good luck!'

The pilots gave a soft cheer as they threw down what they were doing and raced across to the hangars, where the mechanics already had the Hurricanes lined up and waiting. The pilots climbed into their cockpits, fixed their parachutes and started the engines. They had practised this for weeks.

Paul took off after his wing commander and flew above and behind the officer's starboard wing for protection.

'The lads from Coastal Command have had a pop at them,' the wing commander told his squadron. 'But don't worry, there are still plenty left for us to shoot down.'

The Firbeck Hurricanes climbed steeply and headed for Sheffield. Barrage balloons shone in the brilliant moonlight and the oily River Don looked like a silver ribbon down below. Searchlights were slicing the sky and some nervous anti-aircraft gunners on the ground in Sheffield were already sending out explosive bursts, even though the Luftwaffe bombers were still a quarter of an hour away.

'Idiots,' the Wing Commander said over the radio. 'I hope someone stops that before they hit a Hurricane.'

The squadron circled and waited. Suddenly the radio crackled into life.

'I see them, sir,' Bronisław Maniak shouted. 'Heading this way from east-south-east – looks like Alexander the Crystal Seer was right!'

35

Sheffield, England
12 December 1940

Everyone we saw in the streets seemed to be the Blackout Burglar. A woman hurried along, pushing an empty pram.

'That would be a good place to hide your loot,' Sally said.

A coalman was delivering sacks of coal on his cart and tipping them into the hatches of the coal sheds in back yards. The horse's breath steamed in the freezing air. Its droppings steamed on the cobbles.

A man hurried out of his house to scoop up the horse-droppings into a paper bag. 'Nice bit of manure for me leeks,' he said. 'Dig for victory!'

'A coalman could make a good cover for a burglar,' Sally said.

We reached the end of Mrs Grimley's lane and huddled in the shadow of a gateway. At least it was out of the cold wind, but still my hands were freezing.

We heard Hurricanes flying overhead – I knew the engine sounds. There were flashes from the anti-aircraft guns on the ground. I groaned. 'Don't they know an RAF plane when they hear one?'

People on the streets were running for home. 'It's all right,' I told a frightened girl from Sally's class. 'They're our planes. It's not a raid.'

The girl looked at me with a fierce scowl. 'Those anti-aircraft shells explode in the sky and bits of metal fall down. If one of them lands on you, then you're dead. I'm not running from the planes – I'm running from our own shells. And if you had half a brain, you'd do the same.' Then she ran off.

Sally smothered her laughter in her grubby little hands. 'If you had half a brain, Billy Thomas! Sounds as if Marjorie knows you as well as I do!'

'Shut up,' I said, as we turned into the back of Jubilee Terrace.

'Put out the light,' Warden Crane shouted, and his voice echoed down the walls of the alley. He seemed to enjoy the sound of his own voice. '"And all our yesterdays have lighted fools the way to dusty death . . ."' he began to recite.

The boxes that held our gas masks were a pale cardboard and they caught the bright moonlight. Warden Crane saw us and strolled over. 'Hello, young Thomases,' he said.

He was going to ask us what we were up to. I had to take his mind off the question. 'What was that you were saying about dusty death?' I asked quickly.

He lifted his face to the moon. 'Ah, Shakespeare again. "Life's but a walking shadow . . ." and talking of shadows, what were you doing in the shadows?'

'Which play?' I asked.

The warden frowned. 'That is a good question. It's a play called *Macbeth*, and they say it is cursed. Theatres have burned down, accidents have happened. In fact,' he said in a low voice, 'it's unlucky to recite the words of the play or even speak its name. Actors usually call it "The Scottish Play".'

'Oh, Mr Crane!' I cried. 'Does that mean you'll be cursed?'

'I hope not. The curse is only supposed to work when you speak the words of . . . erm . . . the Scottish Play . . . inside a theatre. But who knows? Maybe tonight I'll have an accident and that'll teach me.'

Before he could get back to asking us what we were up to, we heard the low drone of the siren as it started its warning wail.

I glanced at Sally. It was what we were expecting. A false alarm to get the people out of their houses. All we had to do was walk around the block and return to our hiding place when everyone was in the shelter – everyone except the Blackout Burglar.

The navy sky was carved with the golden rods of searchlights. Doors began to open and people walked out grumbling into the dark.

'Another false alarm,' a woman's voice said.

'Never mind, Ma, there's nothing good on the radio,' a boy replied. 'And I can play cards with the other lads.'

'Hurry along,' Warden Crane shouted. 'And turn

out your lights *before* you open your doors. There's more light in this street than at the Sheffield Opera House. I'll fine the lot of you!'

'Aye, we don't want to help them invisible German bombers, do we?' a woman shouted back.

I heard the planes before anyone else. 'Listen!' I shouted. 'There really *are* planes up there.'

'They'll be the Hurricanes from Firbeck,' an old man said.

I strained my ears. The sound was like a double drumbeat – *pock-a, pock-a, pock-a, pock-a.* That's the way German aircraft engines sounded. The British planes just made a steady *brrrr* noise.

'They're German,' I said. 'It's not a false alarm this time.'

People began to shout and their shoes clattered on the cobbles as they ran. The sound of the shoes was joined by the banging of the guns trying to shoot down the attackers. Brilliant lights lit up the sky.

'Parachute flares,' I told Sally.

She raised her pale face. 'What do we do, Billy?'

A car skidded around the corner and its engine screamed as the driver raced for a shelter. 'A Lanchester,' I said. 'It's Mr Cutter's car – what's he doing out driving at night?'

The rumble of engines was growing louder and flashes of orange light were followed by claps of thunder that rattled the gates in the alley. People were screaming and fire-engine bells could be heard in the distance. Dogs barked in panic and the pop of anti-aircraft shells stopped, only to be replaced by the rattle of our fighter planes' cannon, invisible in the glowing sky.

'Let's get to a shelter,' I said.

'We'll miss the burglar,' Sally shouted.

'No – the burglar only goes out when he's phoned in a false alarm. He wouldn't be daft enough to go out in a real raid.'

'Maybe,' Sally said.

We turned and ran.

36

Over Firbeck, England
12 December 1940

The Firbeck wing commander turned to meet the enemy and his squadron of Hurricanes followed. The bomber's moon that helped the Luftwaffe bombers see their targets also let the Hurricanes see the bombers.

Flashes sparked across the sky as Spitfires from Group 12 at Cranwell near Lincoln were already attacking. Tracer bullets ran from the fighters to the bombers in four-second streams and the fire was returned by the gunners in the enemy planes.

The bombers flew on, as if they were rhinos being attacked by annoying but feeble wasps. Still, as Paul drew nearer, he could see a Dornier with one of its engines streaming smoke. The pilot turned it to make a run back to a German airfield, but two Spitfires pounced and drove it down.

'Attack the formation to the north,' the squadron leader said. 'Keep out of the way of the Cranwell Spits to the south.'

Paul saw his commander begin to dive towards the leading Heinkel He 111 and he followed. Just when he thought he had the enemy in his sights, he saw flashes of cannon-fire coming from the top gunner and heading straight towards him. He kicked the rudder on the Hurricane and slid sideways in a panic, then found himself past the German and diving towards another group.

He'd already lost touch with his wing commander and there was no chance of joining him again in the darkness. Again, a top gunner spotted Paul and sent a volcano stream of canon shells towards him. This time the pilot held his nerve. He side-slipped just enough to avoid the enemy fire, then turned to get the bomber in his sights. He managed a one-second burst of fire that made the Hurricane shudder, then he pulled back the joystick to soar upwards and aim for the belly of another bomber, a black shape against the purple sky.

Time after time Paul attacked, but never managed more than two seconds on target and none of the enemy seemed hurt by his wasp stings. Still the black shapes rolled forward, unstoppable as the tide.

He finally found a Dornier whose gunner wasn't firing – maybe he had been killed in a previous attack, maybe his cannons were jammed, or maybe he was out of ammunition. Paul lined up his Hurricane for a killing run. He dived, pressed the firing button and waited for the shots to shake his plane.

Nothing.

He had run out of ammunition. Paul pushed the nose of the Hurricane down. He rushed over the silver fields and found the glittering Don. From there, he worked out the position of Firbeck.

Sheffield was starting to burn. The first bombers had dropped their explosives and now the incendiaries – the flame-makers – were doing their work. The fires would light the way for the next flight of bombers and the Spitfires and Hurricanes would not be able to stop them all from getting through.

Paul Grimley's landing on the dark airstrip was rough enough to smash a Spitfire's undercarriage, but the Hurricane was tougher and he bounced and careered over the grass till he was rolling quickly towards the hangars. He threw back the canopy and shouted at the engineers, 'More ammunition and refuel her.'

'There are a few holes in her, sir,' the engineer said, walking around the hot, hissing plane.

'Can they be fixed?'

'Give me an hour, sir.'

Paul nodded and went over to the canteen for a strong, sweet tea. Sheffield glowed crimson and orange against the skyline twenty miles away. By the time he'd finished his tea, more Hurricanes were landing and rolling towards the hangar.

The wing commander was one of the last to land. 'Sheffield air-raid defence says the bombing has stopped for now. Radar stations are warning a second flight of a hundred planes is about fifty miles east. We take off as soon as they're in range.'

'Any casualties?' someone asked.

'We've lost three planes – won't know if the pilots crash-landed or bailed out till tomorrow morning. But Jerry lost more. At least twenty were sent down or driven back home. Let's aim to get more next time. Put up your feet, grab something to eat and be ready to go in an hour.

Sheffield, England
12 December 1940

Sally and I slipped out of the shelter after that first attack. It was quieter now, though we heard the odd explosion in the distance as a bomb with a timer fuse went off.

We ran through the streets to check on our suspects.

The door to Mrs Haddock's sweet shop stood open and the woman was standing in the doorway looking up. 'You need to get to a shelter, Mrs Haddock,' Sally told her.

The old woman stayed staring at the sky. 'I have a Morrison shelter in the kitchen. If they start getting close I'll go under there.'

'It's not as good as a proper shelter,' a man said.

We looked around to see Sergeant Proctor standing across the street. He was carrying a rifle and his face was as grey as the pavement.

'She won't go,' Sally told him.

'That may be, but you two kids should be there,' the man said.

As we turned to head for the Stanhope Street shelter, the Home Guard man said, 'Not that way – keep away from the houses. If there's a blast, you'll be hit by flying bricks and glass and slates off the roofs. Go across to Attercliffe Common – it will take longer, but it's safer. Here, I'll come with you.'

The common was bleak and overgrown with damp weeds. The sky all around was glowing orange as Sheffield burned.

37

Over Sheffield, England
12 December 1940

Ernst Weiss spoke into his microphone mask. 'We are through Group 12 fighter defences. We have light damage, but not enough to stop us dropping our bombs on the target. I can see the fires from the first wave ahead. Everyone in position for the bombing run?'

'Yes, sir,' came the crew voices over the radio.

'Ready for Group 13 fighters, Werner?'

'Ready, Ernst,' the upper gunner replied.

'Good lad. You look after us.'

'Yes, sir.'

'Four minutes to target,' the navigator said.

A searchlight combed the sky and for a moment it caught Ernst Weiss's Heinkel. Shells from the anti-aircraft guns rose towards them, but the gunners on the ground had miscalculated the height and they exploded a thousand feet below.

'The lead plane is making its run!' Ernst said. 'Bomb doors open!'

'Fighter on the port wing!' the gunner shouted over the radio.

'It's too late to avoid him, Werner – we're on our bombing run. You'll have to deal with it.'

'Yes, sir.'

Ernst Weiss glanced to his left. He felt the plane tremble and saw the golden stream of shells as the gunner fired. He turned back to make sure he was on the right flight path – a path that would take them over the factories to the east of the city if the X-Gerat system was working.

Suddenly, the Heinkel bucked like a wild horse. For four long seconds it was pushed across the sky as Hurricane shells tore into it. Then the British fighter was past. Ernst set his plane as straight as he could but there was a problem with the starboard wing. A white mist was streaming away from it and there was little power from the propeller on that side.

'Starboard fuel tank hit – probably the propeller, too,' the engineer reported.

'And Werner? Did you hit him?' Ernst asked. 'Come in, Werner. Werner?'

There was no reply.

When Paul Grimley had lifted his Hurricane off Firbeck airfield to meet the second wave of planes, it had felt heavy with fuel and shells.

The German bombers were almost upon them by the time the Hurricanes had climbed high enough to touch the moon. With a tilt of the flight commander's wings, they dived at the oncoming planes.

Paul was calm now. When he saw a target, he decided to stick with it till he had finished it off.

No more scattering cannon shells among the monstrous fleet. 'Send one Jerry down,' he muttered to himself, 'then go after the next one.'

The curve of the River Don showed they were near the eastern edge of the city. He had to bring down one Heinkel before it dropped its bombs – dropped them on his mother's house, if they carried on this course.

Paul picked his victim, gathered speed, and swung round to attack from the port side. The upper gunner saw him and sent a wave of tracers in his direction. They were wide of his starboard wing, so he carried straight on.

Slowly, the tracer began to curve towards him. Paul held his nerve. When the Heinkel filled his sights, he pressed the trigger on his own cannon.

One second.

Enemy shells found his bullet-proof screen and cracked off into the night.

Two seconds.

He saw puffs of smoke come from the German's gun turret.

Three seconds.

The enemy cannon stopped firing.

Four seconds.

His shells ripped into the Heinkel's starboard wing, puncturing the fuel tanks and sparking splinters off the starboard propeller.

He stopped firing as he sped over the enemy

bomber. It was wounded but not dead. He soared into the sky, looked around and turned in a wide circle.

'Werner is . . . wounded, and our plane has taken light damage,' Ernst Weiss told the crew. 'Let's drop our load and get the hell out of here.'

'We're a little north-west of the target,' the navigator said. 'For some reason, the beam has taken us away from the factories.'

'Never mind that. We need to get rid of the bombs. Bomb doors open . . . and hurry. If that Hurricane comes back, he'll shoot us like fish in a bowl.'

In the bomb bay, Manfred and Irena sat silent and cold, unsure of where they were or when the girl would have to jump. Suddenly, there was a clank and the doors in the floor began to open. The freezing air hit them like a glacier wall and made breathing hard.

Manfred reached out and wrapped an arm around the girl's shoulders; bones and hunger, held together with a fierce will to survive.

The bomb-aimer pulled a lever and, one by one, the bombs clanked into place and dropped from the plane. In the faintest of lights, Manfred saw Hansl's chalked message roll past him: 'This one is for you, Tommy.'

With the upper gunner dead, Paul Grimley knew the Heinkel was a safe target on the next run.

As he turned and fixed the enemy bomber in his

sights, he saw dark shapes falling from beneath the Heinkel and flashes appearing on the ground.

'Damn you!' the pilot screamed. 'You've got your bombs away, but you won't get home, Jerry.'

Attercliffe Common, Sheffield, England
12 December 1940

As we reached the grassy area, we saw a blinding flash just over the streets we had left. Sergeant Proctor put an arm around each of us and threw us into the deep, damp grass. A moment later, there was a crack like thunder and a blast of hot air roared over our heads. It was followed by a storm of whistling metal and bricks. Some dropped near us with deadly thumps but none touched us.

At last, the noise and rain of steel died. We raised our heads. There was a gap in the skyline where rows of houses had been.

'A mine,' Sergeant Proctor groaned. 'It explodes in the air just above the rooftops and wrecks the houses, but I can't see any fire. I hope those people got to the shelters in time. And that's where you two need to be.'

I was shaking and bruised and my legs felt like water as I struggled to my feet. I wasn't sure which way the Stanhope Street shelter was. All I could see were the flashes in the sky and the glowing ring of fire on the horizon.

'Come on, son,' Sergeant Proctor said. In the faint light, I could see he was shaking and his face was streaked with mud.

Sally rose to her feet and looked as confused as me. The Home Guard pointed to the right. 'This way.'

We set off on trembling legs, stumbling over some of the bricks that had been scattered onto the common. One piece of wall was the size of a door. If that had landed on me, I wouldn't be walking to the shelter now.

Over Attercliffe Common, Sheffield, England
12 December 1940

Paul Grimley aimed his Hurricane at the Heinkel again. The pilot was trying to turn it now, banking away from the fires below and running for home. One of its engines was smoking and it was already losing height.

With no upper gunner to worry him, Paul was able to fly steadily behind the slow bomber and take aim at the one good engine on the port side.

One second.

The shells flew too high. He tipped the control stick forward as he kept a thumb on the button on the top.

Two seconds.

Sparks appeared on the enemy's port wing.

Three seconds.

Smoke and fuel poured from the wing.

Four seconds.

The shells set fire to the escaping fuel and a flower of flame appeared.

'You won't be going home tonight, Jerry,' Paul said as he turned back to Firbeck.

Ernst felt the controls go limp in his hands. There was no power to pull him out of the shallow dive – a dive that would take them into the dark fields of England in five minutes.

'Bail out,' he ordered and unfastened himself from the seat. He felt the dive go a little steeper as the plane lurched around and headed back to the city it had just bombed.

The crew had no radios now, but Ernst gave hand signals for them to open the door. One at a time, he pointed to the men to jump into the night.

He glanced over his shoulder and followed. He pulled on the rip-cord of his parachute and looked up to check that it was opening. He knew Werner wouldn't be bailing out. Werner, the young, happy man who enjoyed playing the piano back at base. Werner, his friend, who had been so full of life and was now dead.

Ernst's head was so full of Werner, he hadn't been thinking about the most important person on the plane.

In the moments before he pulled his rip-cord to open the parachute, he saw the Heinkel pass over his head, he saw the open bomb doors . . . and he remembered.

'Manfred!' he screamed. 'Manfred!' But his screams were lost in the shadows.

Manfred and Irena felt the plane dying and watched as the bomb-aimer struggled towards the crew doors at the front.

The fire from the port engine lit their faces orange but did nothing to warm them. Manfred leaned forward and looked through the bomb bay. He saw parachutes open like mushrooms and vanish behind the diving plane.

'We are going to crash,' he shouted over the whine of the wounded engine. 'The crew have bailed out. Save yourself, Irena. Jump.'

'You?'

'I don't have a parachute,' he said. 'Don't worry about me. I'll be dying for Herr Hitler and the Fatherland. This is not your war. Jump!'

'You would not be here if you had not tried to help me,' Irena said. Her lips were frozen and it was hard for her to speak.

The plane lurched again. 'If you don't jump soon, we'll be too low. We'll both die,' Manfred argued. 'What's the sense in that?'

Irena rose to her legs and pulled Manfred up after

her. They teetered on the edge of the open doors with the bomb-torn city flashing below. She placed Manfred's arms around her neck. 'Hang on tight,' she said then leaned sideways so they toppled into the smoke-stained sky. Her spy-hat flew off and her fine hair streamed in the wind.

Suddenly, the air went quiet. Irena tugged at the rip-cord and the parachute flared above them. Then she wrapped her arms around the boy's waist and held him close.

They fell as if in a dark dream.

38

Attercliffe Common, Sheffield, England
12 December 1940

Sally stopped so quickly I ran into the back of her. 'Keep going,' I shouted. 'What's wrong?'

My sister didn't reply. She just raised a hand and pointed up at the sky. In the flashes of light, we could make out a green parachute.

'German,' Sergeant Proctor said and pulled back the bolt on his rifle to load it.

'It could be one of our Hurricane pilots baling out,' I said.

'The British use white parachutes. No, it's either a German aircrew . . . or a spy. This is my job – shooting spies is what the Home Guard was made for.'

He put the rifle to his shoulder and took aim. In the glow of the fires, I saw the rifle was shaking.

A bundle at the end of the parachute hit the ground and the silk of the chute slowly collapsed like a punctured football. The bundle beneath seemed to split in two.

'*Hände hoch*!' Sergeant Proctor shouted. 'Hands up, or I shoot. Throw down your weapon. I have you covered.'

A small figure picked itself up and looked at us. It was a girl as small as Sally, as pale and calm as the distant moon. She raised her hands over her head. As I drew closer, I saw she was a fierce-eyed, crop-haired, starve-faced, scarecrow-clothed, ice-block-cold, unafraid child.

Then a second figure rose from the grass to stand beside her. It was a boy about my age with a round, dazed face.

'The fiends!' the Home Guard cried. 'They're not sending nuns to kill us – they're sending children.'

'They're just kids,' Sally said. 'They can't do any harm.'

'Trained assassins, they are. Trained to kill with their bare hands. I bet they have daggers hidden in their socks, ready to stab us as soon as we turn our backs.'

My dazed head was clearing and I looked carefully at the boy and the girl. 'I don't think so.'

'Hitler Youth, they call the boys. And League of German Girls. They're like boy scouts only with machine guns hidden in their socks.'

'Machine guns?' Sally jeered. 'The girl's too skinny to have a *pencil* in her sock.'

The wave of bombers seemed to have passed. The sky was quieter now, but the fire-engine bells and the rumble of tumbling buildings went on around us. We were lit by the amber glow of the distant fires. The German children didn't look much like storm troopers to me.

The boy looked at the girl and spoke in German. I found out later what they had been saying.

'So, Irena, you have come all this way to England only for them to shoot you!'

'We aren't dead yet, Manfred.'

'If those two English children landed in Germany, our army would shoot them,' he said.

'But I am not German,' she reminded him. 'I am Polish. The Poles have no war with the British.'

'I think we should run for it. That man is shaking so much he won't hit us if we run into the dark.'

'No, Manfred. We are lost and alone. Trust me. I speak a little English. Let me talk to them – you must pretend you are Polish, too.'

'An under-human? Me?'

'A live under-human or a dead German. Which would you prefer?' she asked.

'Go ahead,' he said.

The girl turned to us. 'We are Polish. I am Irena, this is Manfred. We were prisoners in Germany. Dachau prison camp. We escape. We fly to England. We jump out with the bombs.'

'Ha!' Sergeant Proctor snorted. 'We know the German tricks. They give you a cover story.'

The girl lowered her hands. Sergeant Proctor jerked his rifle back up towards her and clattered the bolt back to check there was a bullet ready to fire. 'Hands up! *Hände hoch!*'

She didn't obey. Instead, she stepped towards us, lifted her chin and began to sing. We all knew the song so well. They sang it in the shelters and Vera Lynn sang it on the radio, we sang it in school assembly and the girls even sang it in the school yard as a skipping song. No one – not even Vera Lynn – ever sang it with a voice so sweet it could melt a heart of steel.

'There'll always be an England
While there's a country lane,
Wherever there's a cottage small
Beside a field of grain.
There'll always be an England
While there's a busy street,
Wherever there's a turning wheel
A million marching feet.'

Suddenly, I heard two more voices join in and sing. The shrill voice of my sister and the creaking voice of Sergeant Proctor. By the last two lines, I found myself trying to join in, but my throat was full of swallowed tears.

'There'll always be an England,
And England shall be free
If England means as much to you
As England means to me.'

The girl stopped and for a few moments the war stopped. The Home Guard didn't have a heart of steel – or if he had, it was melting like the steel in the furnaces down at Tinsley.

'No, lass, the Hitler Youth could teach you the words,' Sergeant Proctor said. 'But they couldn't teach you to sing it like that – as if you meant it. Welcome to England . . . friends.' He rested his rifle on the ground so he could pull a handkerchief from his pocket and blow his nose. 'Let's get you to a shelter till the raid is over and sort you out.'

The girl turned and smiled at the boy who had landed with her. 'It will be all right, Manfred. They will care for us. We are with friends.'

39

We walked off the common and back onto Attercliffe Road. A group of people were walking up the road towards us. One ran forward and cried, 'Billy? Sally? Why aren't you in the shelter?'

It was Dad, but his uniform was torn and his hands and face spattered with blood.

'What's happened? Why aren't you at Firbeck?'

'One of the first bombs wrecked the tram lines and blew in the windows of the tram. There was no way forward, so we thought we might as well come back and help,' he explained.

'Fire the anti-aircraft guns?' I asked.

'No, lad, find people in the rubble. A warden said he had a call from the town centre. The cathedral's been wrecked while people were in there praying. Any fit men are needed to look for people buried under the mess. Now get yourselves to Stanhope Street shelter as fast as you can,' he said and hurried off in the direction of the town.

'Hang on,' Sergeant Proctor called after him. 'I'm coming with you! Can you find your way to the shelter?' he asked us.

'Blindfolded,' Sally told him.

We were left to make our way to safety with the other children. I explained to Irena what we were going to do and she told Manfred. Another wave of bombers began to stream over the city and Sally and I jumped every time there was a noise, waiting for the blast that would spread us over the road like jam. Yet Irena was as calm as a sleepwalker. Her eyes were alive, but she walked steadily and her courage made us fearless, too.

'Look, Manfred,' she said. 'In Germany, you are made to starve. In England, they give away free food on street corners!'

I asked what she was saying and had to explain, 'That's not free food – it's waste food. That's a pig-bin.'

She shook her head. 'In Dachau camp, that is good food. There are no waste-food bins in Dachau camp.'

We walked on through streets as moon-bright, bomb-lit, fire-coloured, rose-skied as daylight.

The shelter was jammed. Even though it was freezing outside, inside it was steaming hot as there were so many people. Some of the Women's Voluntary Service were serving tea and sandwiches.

At last, Irena began to show some feeling. She gazed on the sandwich pile – fish paste, a few cheese and some made with slices of Spam.

'All that food,' she breathed and spoke in English. 'Look, Manfred, you think you Germans are starving the British to death, but they have more food than a king in a palace!'

'I thought Manfred was Polish,' Sally said quickly.

Irena screwed up her face, cross with herself for her slip. 'He is Polish now,' she said and explained no more. When we reached the front of the queue, she took a plate and a sandwich. Manfred said something sharply as she placed it to her lips.

'What is he saying?' I asked.

'He said I must not eat too fast. I will be sick. I have not had so much food for many months.'

'One sandwich?' Sally asked.

Irena shrugged. 'A little turnip soup twice a day. A small piece of bread. Just enough to keep me alive – not enough to give me the strength to escape.'

'But you did,' I said as I chewed on a disgusting fish-paste sandwich and pulled a bone out of my teeth.

She looked at me and shook her head in wonder. 'I did,' she said. 'I really did.' And her eyes filled with tears.

Manfred ate silently and his eyes darted around the room, afraid.

I pointed a finger at my chest. 'Me, Billy.' I pointed at him. 'Manfred?'

He nodded. He was going to be hard work to talk to, but just then our mum came along and smothered us in hugs. 'I thought you were at one of the other shelters!' she cried.

'We were,' Sally lied. 'But we were worried about you so we came here.' Then she explained how we'd met Irena and Manfred on the common and seen Dad.

Mum looked at the foreign children. 'Things must be bad in Germany if you took such a risk to escape,' she said. 'But you're safe now. There are a lot of Polish pilots at Firbeck air base. They'll be happy to look after you. We'll get you there as soon as this raid is over and we're all cleared up.'

The rest of that night passed like a bad dream. It is jumbled in my memory because we kept falling asleep in the warm fug. We found a corner and sat on blankets. Irena rested her head on Manfred's shoulder and fell asleep first. He looked at her with a strange mixture of pain and tenderness before he, too, fell asleep. Sally was snoring soon after and I couldn't keep my eyes open, either.

At around two in the morning, there was a lot of noise and I rubbed my eyes to see Mum sitting next to me on the floor, supping tea from a white enamel mug.

'What's happening?' I asked.

'Another attack. One of the wardens from the post next door says a bomb landed on the Marple Hotel near the centre of town. It's Thursday night – there will have been a lot of people there dancing. Poor, poor people . . . and their families. Your dad's in that part of –' She tailed off.

'Part of what?' I asked.

'Nothing, Billy. Go back to sleep,' she said. And I did.

We were woken by the last raid around three in the morning. This time, the bombs seemed further away but still they shook the shelter. Manfred began to mutter in his sleep. '*Eins*. . .' and then as the second bomb exploded, '*zwei*. . .' then, '*drei*. . .' then, '*vier* . . .' and finally, '*fünf*. . .'

Irena had tried to place a hand over his mouth. 'Hush, Manfred!'

'What's he doing?' I asked.

'Counting – the bombs come in racks of five. They are released, one rack at a time, and the bombs fall in fives. When you hear number five, you know you're safe for a while.'

'And if you don't hear five?'

'You probably don't hear it because you are dead,' Irena shrugged, turned over and went back to sleep.

I fell asleep counting bombs instead of sheep that nightmare night.

40

Sheffield, England
13 December 1940

We stepped out of the shelter the next morning. The air was filled with a dusty haze of smashed bricks and cement and the sharp scent of burning wood. Somehow it was better than the scent of the toilet buckets and the tobacco smoke inside the shelter.

We stood outside our house. Windows were cracked and a chimney pot leaned at a crazy angle, but we were the lucky ones.

In the next street, houses lay shattered and smoking. Home Guard and ARP men crawled over the rubble like beetles.

Manfred's face was filled with pain and he said something to Irena. She turned to us.

'Manfred's grandpa had a house damaged by bombs. He says we have to search quickly. If you leave it too long, the people inside will die.'

I looked at Sally. 'I don't suppose there will be any school today. Let's do what we can.'

Dad was walking down the street towards us. His cuts had not been patched and his hands were torn and bleeding. 'You're all safe, thank God,' he said. 'I've been to the Marple Hotel. It took a direct hit.'

'Anyone inside?' Mum asked.

'Just before eleven, a bomb flattened the C&A Modes store across the road from the Marple. Some people were hurt, so they all took shelter in the cellars of the Marple. An hour later, a bomb went clean through the hotel roof, through seven stories of rooms and bars, and brought the whole lot down on the poor souls in the cellars. It'll take a week to get them out.'

'Alive?' I asked.

Dad just shook his head. 'One or two, if they're lucky. But there must have been a hundred poor beggars inside. We started digging, but it was hopeless. Angel Street and King Street are just blown away.' He looked up at the sky. 'I thought they were supposed to be aiming for the factories, not people out having a dance. How come so many bombs hit the town centre, everyone's asking. What a bloody war.'

Mum wrapped an arm around his shoulder and led him back home to tend to his wounds. We four children stood and looked at a stream of people walking up the road with shovels and saws, buckets and crowbars. We followed as they headed towards Jubilee Terrace. The rescuers were milling around the end of Mrs Grimley's street.

'The street was clear, Mrs Grimley,' Sergeant Proctor of the Home Guard was saying wearily. 'We checked the names of everyone in this street and they were all in the shelter. There's nobody to dig out here.'

'I tell you, I came back at first light and I heard a

voice,' she said and jabbed him with a bony finger. 'I'm not deaf and I'm not daft, Mr Proctor.'

We looked up at the house. The end wall had collapsed into the roadway. The roof had sunk down on its thick beams and through the broken slates we could see the flowered wallpaper of her bedroom and one corner of an iron bed.

Sally leaned towards me. 'If it's not someone from the street then you know who it must be.'

'The Blackout Burglar!' I said. 'We didn't catch him, but it looks like the Luftwaffe did.'

Beneath the ruined wall of Mrs Grimley's house, I could make out the crushed remains of a car. The badge on the front was covered in dust. I brushed it away and saw that it was a Lanchester.

I could have loved that car. Once, in the school yard, I sneaked the door open and looked inside the ice-black, shiny-leather-scented, walnut-chrome, smooth-dialled, polished work of art made from Sheffield steel. When you're young, the death of a car matters as much as the death of a man. When you grow older, you learn that a car can be replaced but a person never can.

'The Blackout Burglar,' I said. 'It was Mr Cutter, our history teacher. He parked here to go inside the house but the wall fell on the car and crushed him,' I explained.

'If he's in there, then there's no point wasting time

digging him out,' Sergeant Proctor said. 'He'll be flat as a hedgehog on the road. We have to find the living ones that we can save.'

The men with shovels and spades nodded and moved on to the next street.

'Mrs Grimley heard him moan,' I said. 'We have to try.'

'You're right, lad,' the old woman said.

Manfred and Irena seemed eager to help and they began to pull away the broken bricks from the roof of the car. Manfred passed them to Irena and she threw them aside with more strength than those pipe-cleaner arms should have had.

'You don't want to see this,' I said to Sally. 'Go home.'

'Listen, Dr Watson, I have been tracking the Blackout Burglar for months. I want to see him.' She stood beside Irena. The Polish girl was older than my sister but no bigger. They could have been sisters and worked side by side like two friends playing with dolls.

At last, Manfred pulled a few bricks from the smashed windscreen and made a hole. The dusty light streamed in. He looked at us with a puzzled face. He shook his head.

Sally scrambled over the bonnet and looked inside. 'No way!' she cried.

'Is it really horrible, Sal?' I asked.

'No – it's really empty!'

'My car!' came a voice from behind me. We swung around to see Mr Cutter, Hitler-moustache bristling, looking at the Lanchester with a pained expression on his face. Mrs Haddock stood next to him.

'You shouldn't have been out last night,' she said.

'You told me to meet you!' he argued fiercely. It was the voice he used when he was cross with us boys. 'As soon as I heard the siren, I parked up and headed for the shelter up the road.'

'And where are my chocolates?' the old woman squawked. 'I stayed in my shop through all the bombing, waiting for you.'

The old policeman, Constable Anderson, who'd visited our house the month before was suddenly by our side. He listened with interest as my history teacher said, 'The chocolates are in the boot of the car, of course. You didn't expect me to deliver them in the middle of an air raid, did you?'

'Get them out,' the old woman said.

'No, leave them,' the policeman said. 'It's evidence.'

The teacher turned sharply and almost fell on his backside. 'Evidence?'

'Is this your car, sir?'

'Well, it was . . .'

'So, if we find black-market goods in the boot, you'll have a bit of explaining to do.'

'Ah . . . no . . . I can explain.'

'And your name is?'

'Cutter!' I cried. 'Mr Cutter. He's a history teacher at our school.'

The policeman made a note and took down the miserable man's address. 'Once we have all the people out of this mess, we'll take a look at the car. Then I'll be paying you a little visit, Mr Cutter. And what is your name, madam?' he asked, turning to the owner of the sweet shop.

'My name? What you want my name for? I've done nowt. I've never even seen this feller in me life, have I?' she asked.

'No, Mrs Haddock, never,' the teacher said savagely and walked off down the dusty street.

'Haddock – fish seller, are you?' Constable Anderson joked. 'Let's go and have a look at your stock, shall we? See if everything's properly paid for. Check your ration books.'

'She is a dark horse,' said the vicar, Mr Treadwell, who had suddenly appeared.

'Morning, sir,' the policeman said and tapped the front of his helmet in salute.

'Good morning, officer. I heard there were injured and dying in this street and I've come to offer them the comfort of God's word.'

'Or he's come to look for the comfort of Mrs Grimley's money,' I said to Sally. 'Treadwell's the Blackout Burglar – I always said it!'

'Did you?' Sally asked. She turned to her new friend, Irena. 'My brother and I are detectives, you know. I am the top 'tec – Sherlock Holmes – and he is my assistant. I'm never wrong and he's never right.'

Irena gave the first smile I'd ever seen on her pinched face. 'Boys are usually wrong. Manfred was wrong. But he is learning.'

Mrs Grimley was arguing with the constable. 'So if it wasn't the teacher in his car, who did I hear groaning?'

'There are no dead or wounded in this street. The Home Guard just told me,' Constable Anderson said.

'If he wasn't in the car, he must be in the ruin of my house,' the old woman said and stamped her clog on the cobbles.

The broken bricks made a rough ramp up to Mrs Grimley's bedroom. Vicar Treadwell looked up eagerly. 'I could go up and see,' he offered.

'No point taking that sort of risk, sir,' the policeman told him. 'That roof could collapse.'

'He wants the money!' I whispered to Sally, and explained quickly to Irena how we'd been hunting the Blackout Burglar.

'Your priest? A thief?' Irena asked.

'Looks like it,' I said.

And then I heard the soft groan. It came from the open bedroom. A piece of broken brick moved.

'There *is* someone up there!' I cried.

'I told you, I told you,' Mrs Grimley crowed.

'We'll get a team here as soon as possible,' Constable Anderson said. 'I'll go to the police box and put a call through. There's so many lost in the ruins this morning, it could take a while.'

'We have to help him *now*!' I argued.

The policeman shook his head. He climbed a few steps up the ramp of rubble towards the bedroom but it crumbled under his feet. 'I could bring the lot down. Finish him off. No, I'm just too heavy.'

'I'm not,' Irena said and she was halfway up before the constable could turn round. He called for her to come back down, but he might as well have asked a Nazi bomb to stop falling. 'Where's that girl's gas mask?' he grumbled.

'Lost it in the bombing,' Sally said quickly.

Irena began to gently lift bricks and throw them down into the street. 'There is a man here,' she said.

'You need help,' Sally called and followed Irena up to the bedroom. Mum would kill me if she knew I'd let my sister climb into danger.

'Ohhhh!' I groaned. 'I'll have to help her,' I said to Manfred.

He didn't speak English but he seemed to understand. We joined hands and helped one another up through the slope of broken bricks.

We could make out the navy uniform and the black helmet with ARP on the front. The helmet had saved him. But a beam from the roof lay across his legs and was weighed down with so much rubble the four of us couldn't move it.

The man's face was white with plaster dust, like a statue. He moaned again and opened his eyes. Irena gently brushed away the dust and we could see the long hair curling out from under the helmet.

Sally almost fell backwards and knocked me over. 'Mr Crane? Warden Crane?' she cried.

'Hello, Sally love,' he croaked. 'I don't suppose you have a drink of water?'

'I'll get it!' said Irena, and scrambled down light as a spider to ask the policeman.

'What are you doing here?' I asked.

His pale eyes looked into mine. 'I am the "snapper-up of unconsidered trifles",' he whispered. 'Shakespeare's words for a thief. I came for Mrs Grimley's money.'

'The Blackout Burglar?'

'And a very good burglar,' he chuckled and the laugh brought a bubble of blood to the corner of his mouth. 'Now I have a thousand pounds, I can retire,' he smiled.

'A thousand pounds?'

'Yes, I have it in my hands.'

His arm was stretched out under the bed. I lifted slates and splinters of wood out of the way and looked under the bed. There was a box. I tugged it out.

'Open it,' the warden said.

The cash box was not locked. I lifted the lid. It was full of one-pound notes. Hundreds of them.

'Show me?' Warden Crane said.

He couldn't raise his head with that heavy black helmet.

'"Death, the one appointment we all must keep",' he sighed.

'Shakespeare?'

'No,' Sally said as Irena appeared with a cracked cup filled from the yard tap. 'Not Shakespeare – the great detective, Charlie Chan.'

'I bet he wouldn't have caught the Blackout Burglar – Charlie Chan's not as great as Sally Thomas.'

My sister unfastened the strap and slipped off the warden's helmet. The morning sun streamed onto his face, and the man blinked. He opened his eyes briefly, but now they were looking at something far away. Something we couldn't see.

'Put out the light!' he cried and the blood sprayed up and over the money he had been dying to find. '"Put out the light, and then put out the light."' And the light went out in his eyes.

I looked at Irena, who shook her head. Then only she had the courage to place her fingertips on the warden's eyelids and close them.

We climbed slowly back down to the cobbles, where Constable Anderson stood next to Mrs Grimley.

I handed the blood-spattered money to her.

'I'm an old fool,' she muttered. 'Hoarding my money like some old miser. If I'd put it in the bank, Mr Crane would still be alive. I feel like I killed him!' she sobbed.

'How is he?' the policeman asked me. 'The warden?'

'Dead.'

The policeman nodded. 'It's as well – I'd only have had to arrest him. He'd never have lived with the disgrace. In a lot of ways he was a nice bloke – kind, funny, good company. I'll miss old Tommy.'

'What?' Irena said sharply.

'Old Tommy Crane, the warden.'

'So he was the "Tommy" the bomb was for,' she said.

'What do you mean?' I asked her.

She looked up at Mrs Grimley's weeping face. 'No, you and your money didn't kill him,' the girl said gently. 'He died because it was his time. There was a bomb with his name on it. And when that happens, all the money in the world won't save you.'

The old woman snuffled. 'Do you think so?'

'I know it,' Irena said. 'I learned one thing in Dachau. The dead are gone and past help. We have to do what we can for the living. Let me help you.'

'You?' the old woman said, and couldn't help but smile.

249

'The shelter we were in last night. They have tea,' Irena said and carefully guided the woman away from the ruins of her house.

'A cup of tea,' Mrs Grimley nodded. 'That's the English answer, lass, always.'

Irena nodded. 'And there'll always be an England,' she agreed.

Epilogue

The war went on for another five dreary years. Sheffield was bombed again on 15 December 1940 and in the end over seven hundred people died, 1,500 were injured and 40,000 lost their homes.

But we discovered it was worse in Germany. Dachau went from being a slave camp to a death camp where the Nazis executed thousands of their enemies. By the end, the Germans were so desperate they were arming Hitler Youth with rifles and sending them to defend Adolf Hitler in Berlin. Youths like little Hansl were forced to fight and die. The Russian army over-ran the city in 1945. Hitler shot himself before they could lay their hands on him. Many loyal fighters, like Hansl, were never seen again.

The German bombers wrecked many cities, but they never won the war in the air. The 'Few' of the RAF held out . . . just. By the end of 1940, it was too late for Hitler to invade Britain. By 1941, the Germans were so busy fighting Russia to the east, they didn't have the army spare to attack England to the west. The invasion never came, thanks to the RAF.

And thanks to the Sheffield workers who never stopped working to make the war machines. Bending the X-Gerat radio beam sent the German bombers into the city centre, where those seven hundred died. We didn't know that till years after the war, of course.

251

Many died so the Sheffield factories could win the war. Was it right? You decide – I don't know.

By 1945, Germany had invented new weapons – V1 flying bombs that were harder to stop than bomber planes, and a new Blitz began in the south of England. Sheffield was spared the second Blitz, though it will always remember the first, on that fire-rain night of 12 December 1940.

Some people lived, some died, but we were all changed by the war. Me? I became a policeman, like Dad. Sally always said my greatest case was my first one – catching the Blackout Burglar – but that I'd never have done it without her help. She may be right.

Mrs Grimley was moved to a new house and we never saw her again. Paul Grimley set off to attack the Luftwaffe in the 15 December raid. He chased one of the Junkers over the North Sea and he never returned. They say Mrs Grimley died of a broken heart. Her blood-soaked money did her no good in the end.

Mr Cutter went to prison for a few months for his black-market deals. Of course he lost his job as a teacher. No one cried. Mrs Haddock was spared prison because she was so old, but her shop was closed and never opened again.

But what about Irena? She spent the war with a Polish family at Firbeck, then she left school to become a children's nurse. She married in 1951, but her body was too damaged by Dachau ever to have children of her own. She was always happy to look after Manfred's children and she became their favourite auntie.

For Manfred married a dreadful young woman. A crazy, reckless, skinny, awkward girl called Sally Thomas, though he always called her 'Tommy'. Manfred had been taken in as a Polish boy at Firbeck, too. Of course the Poles knew he wasn't one of them, but Irena argued fiercely for him. 'He saved my life. If there are any good Germans, he is one of them,' she had pleaded.

Pilot Ernst Weiss had the strangest fate. He parachuted safely out of the Heinkel and drifted down to land at Lodge Moor – a prison camp for German prisoners of war. He had a short walk to the gates of the prison, where he spent the rest of the war. Manfred managed to visit him from time to time and they agreed they were both safer in England . . . safe from the revenge of the Gestapo. After the war, they managed to get back to Dachau and find their parents. They were told the American invaders had arrived on 29 April 1945 and set the prisoners free. The horrors they found in Dachau death camp made Sheffield's suffering seem small. The Nazis had built gas chambers there to murder the prisoners.

American soldiers cried when they saw prisoners sorting the shoes of dead children. They were sickened to see prisoners forced to make soap made from the corpses of dead friends. The prisoners executed their guards and kapos. Revenge for murdered friends makes even good people do evil deeds.

The horrors of the Blitz faded, but we never forgot them. Never will.

For many years, Manfred was treated as an enemy, spat at in the streets, only allowed to do badly paid work – clearing the bomb sites, labouring in the steelworks or on the building sites as Sheffield put itself back together. He was German and so the people of Sheffield took their anger about the Blitz out on him.

But people forget. And with Sally by his side no one was allowed to call him 'Nazi' – I think my crazy little sister would have punched them. In time, he went to college and became a teacher – of German, of course. Unlike Mr Cutter, he was one of the most popular teachers in the school. His three children (my two nephews and a niece) are wonderful people and proud of their father, proud of their city, proud of the way it survived the worst the Luftwaffe could deliver.

'There will always be an England,' Irena liked to remind me when we watched the new city rising from the dust-white, rubble-black, charred-brown of the old.

And I am proud of my nephews. For I married but never had children of my own. As I said, Irena couldn't have children. Oh, didn't I mention Irena became my wife? The finest, most loyal and hard-working woman you could ever meet. She never complained about her broken body; to be alive was enough, to be free was more than she'd dreamed of in Dachau.

Of course, she died quite young . . . not even sixty. I suppose this is her story. A tale of how in the darkest of times, with the most evil of people in power, there are some things that will always survive.

No matter how many bodies the Nazis broke, there was one thing they could never break. The human spirit. The spirit of people like Irena. As long as their courage is remembered, their light shines on.

Put out *that* light?

Never.

About the Author

Put out the Light is the 200th book by Terry Deary. He has been writing fiction and non fiction for young readers for over 30 years, selling 25 million books in over 40 languages, and seen many of his books adapted for television.

Terry began work as a professional actor and wrote plays for his theatre company. His first break into becoming a published author came in 1976 when he adapted one of his plays, *The Custard Kid*, as a children's novel and sold it to A & C Black. They continue to publish his books to this day, including the popular **Time Tales** historical fiction series.

For more details of Terry's books, why not visit his website – www.terry-deary.com.